THE FRONTIERSMAN

JOHN LEGG

WOLFPACK
PUBLISHING
— EST 2013 —

WOLFPACK
PUBLISHING
— EST 2013 —

The Frontiersman
by John Legg

Paperback Edition

Wolfpack Publishing
6032 Wheat Penny Avenue
Las Vegas, NV 89122

Paperback ISBN: 978-1-64734-201-2
Ebook ISBN: 978-1-64734-063-6

THE FRONTIERSMAN

For the Ingrams
—Rick, Jo, Ben and Beki—
for all your help, kindness,
and most of all, your
unwavering love and friendship.
I am in your debt.

CHAPTER 1

Linus Hudson and his two Cheyenne companions had a little trouble stopping the twenty-six horses, but they finally managed. He and the two Indians sat on their ponies looking out across the rolling blankness of the prairie.

"These doin's don't shine none with this boy," Hudson grumbled quietly as he tried to figure out what was going on out in the distance.

"You think the fort's burnin'?" Mad Buffalo asked.

Hudson shook his head. "Cain't be that, my friend. That smoke's spread out too far. Hell, looks like it goes on for miles."

"A village?" Whirling Storm asked, worried. He and his companions had been gone a fair long time and many things could have happened in that time.

"Could be, but I cain't recall a time when so many of the People was at the fort at one time. Hell, if that's a village out there, every one of the People must be here. If that's true, it means big trouble." Hudson paused, leaning over the side of his horse to spit tobacco juice into the prairie grass. "Well, shit," he said as he straightened, "we ain't gonna find out settin' here."

The three men moved on at a slow, even pace, driving the horses ahead of them. A mile on, they topped one of the many low rises and could see for some distance. They stopped again and stared. Bent's Fort was a brown smudge on the dim horizon. A little closer and fading away into the distance were tents and streamers of smoke from cookfires.

"Blue coats," Mad Buffalo suddenly said. He was not happy about this. He had encountered soldiers before, both Mexican and American, but never in such numbers.

"There's a heap of them critters, ain't there," Hudson commented dryly. "Wonder what they're doin' hereabouts."

"Don't matter," Mad Buffalo offered. "I'm headin' back to the village." He was growing more and more worried. If this many soldiers had crossed Cheyenne land, there was no telling what devastation they had left behind. "You two can do what you want."

"I don't like to say this, Fierce Bear," Whirling Storm said, using the name the Cheyennes had given their longtime friend, "but I'm goin' with Mad Buffalo."

Hudson nodded, understanding their concerns. He was tempted to go with them. His wife lived in their village and he was as worried about her as Mad Buffalo and Whirling Storm were about their families. But he figured he could do more good down at the fort. He could more easily learn information there and then decide what to do. Besides, if the army had ridden through some of the villages, and he figured Stolen Back Woman was hurt or dead, he could start avenging the loss right away.

"You boys want your ponies now?" Hudson asked after a few moments.

Both Indians nodded. They were very concerned about their families and their people but they had expended considerable effort in getting these horses and wanted them. They trusted Hudson to give them the ponies later, if that's what they wanted, but both were afraid that the soldiers might take them for their own uses. They also worried that they might need the extra horses to help their people if the soldiers had laid waste to some of the Cheyenne villages.

"Cut out the ones you want," Hudson said. He leaned forward, resting his forearms on his saddlehorn. They had long ago agreed that each Cheyenne would take eight horses; Hudson would get ten since he and the Indians considered him the leader of this expedition.

Mad Buffalo and Whirling Storm spent only minutes in culling out the horses they wanted. They were in a hurry to get back to their people, plus they had had plenty of time on the trail to check out which ponies they liked.

Hudson straightened when the two Cheyennes were ready to leave. He could see the worry etched on the Indians' faces. His own mouth was dry with concern. "You'll check on Stolen Back Woman?" he asked quietly.

Both Cheyennes nodded. They raised their right hands, palms out, and Hudson returned the gesture. Then the Indians turned and galloped off with their horses. Hudson watched them for a few seconds, then began driving his own small herd down toward the fort.

He tried to avoid the soldiers' camps as best he could, what with the ten horses and a pack mule. It wasn't easy, but he managed to thread his way through them without event, though he caught a number of curious stares. Finally, he rode through the massive double oak doors of the imposing adobe structure and stopped in the placita.

The place was more crowded than Hudson had ever seen it before. He had worked at the fort for the Saint Vrain Company off and on since the beaver trade had died six years before, and while he had always seen the place buzzing with activity, this was highly unusual. Mexican laborers bustled about and their wives and children wove their way through the throngs of soldiers in the placita, also working hard. Most of the soldiers were doing little but ogling the senoras in their rather revealing outfits. The soldiers had never seen the like of it.

The noise was horrendous, too. Thousands of horses whinnied and snorted, cows lowed and bellowed, chickens cackled, mules brayed loudly in and around the fort. The human activity added to the overall cacophony.

Hudson stopped near the rear of the fort, close to the "arch" through which lay the stockade and some of the workshops. A young, tall, thin Mexican man hurried up, accompanied by two boys.

"Senor Hudson," the Mexican said. "Hola."

"Hola, Pedro. "*¿Como esta usted, amigo?*"

"Bien, senor. Muy bien" Pedro Ramirez smiled tiredly. "Do you remember my sons, Senor Hudson?" he asked, indicating the two boys with him.

Hudson dismounted. "Por supuesto—of course." He touched one boy on the head. "Miguel," he said, then pointed at the other, "and Juan. ¿Como estan ustedes, muchachos?" he asked with a smile.

"Muy bien," the two echoed shyly.

"Should I take your horses, Senor Hudson?" Ramirez asked. He had a heavy accent but he spoke English well.

"Sí, Pedro. Put 'em with the others."

"There are few others, senor," Ramirez said. He looked around slyly to see if anyone was listening. Then he said in conspiratorial tones, "And you might not have these much longer if you leave them here."

"What the hell's that supposed to mean?" Hudson asked, a little confused.

"It's not for me to say, senor."

"You ain't no help."

"All I'll say to you, Senor Hudson, is that you should take these horses away—muy pronto."

Hudson thought about that for a moment. Ramirez's statements just added to the puzzle of what was going on here. It was all strange, very strange. He decided he had to figure it out first. "You know what the hell's goin' on here, Pedro?" he suddenly asked. If anyone knew that, it would be one of the workers like Ramirez. They always seemed to know everything that was going on in the fort.

"I can't say, senor," Ramirez responded flatly.

"Hell, Pedro, you can tell me. We're old amigos. I ain't gonna do nothin' that'll get you in trouble with Bill or the others. You know that."

"Sí, I know that," Ramirez said with a nod. "It's not Senor Bent who will give me trouble if I say anything."

"The soldiers?" Hudson asked.

"They causin' trouble here?"

Ramirez looked around again, worry growing on his face. Then he nodded.

"What kind of trouble, Pedro?"

"I can say no more."

"One more question. You hear any talk about the soldiers ridin' through any of the Cheyenne villages?" Outwardly, there was no sign of his worry.

"I've heard nothing about that, Senor Hudson but nobody tells one such as me anything."

"Buffler shit."

"I can say no more," Ramirez repeated. "Only that you ought to get your horses out of here."

Hudson shook his head. "I got to see what the hell's goin' on first. You know where Bill is?"

Ramirez shook his head. "He could be anywhere these days," he said cryptically.

Hudson nodded. "All right, Pedro. Take the horses away. I'll take my chances. Gracias." He slipped Ramirez a gold coin. "You share that with Miguel and Juan, you hear me," he said gruffly but he winked.

"Si, senor," Ramirez responded, brightening

fractionally. "Gracias." He and his two sons led the horses, including Hudson's saddle horse, off after Hudson had pulled his rifle out of the leather loop on the front of the saddle near the horn.

Hudson turned and headed for the dining room in the left rear corner of the fort. It was as good a place as any to start his search for Bill Bent, one of the three owners of the fort and the one who generally ran it.

The dining room was full of soldiers, a number of whom surrounded Bent at one of the long roughhewn tables. The only reason Hudson knew Bent was there was the sound of the trader's voice. Bent, being barely five-and-a-half-feet tall at best, could not be seen amid the throng of officers.

Hudson was not surprised to see so many soldiers in here, not after he had seen the stretched-out army camps. He was, however, surprised to see that he— and Bent—were the only two nonarmy men. Often there were a bunch of trappers and traders congregating in the fort and in the dining room. Even at this time of the year, when many of those men were out conducting business, there always seemed to be a few of them around. But not this time.

He bulled his way through the soldiers, who didn't think kindly of the action. None said anything, though. Hudson didn't look like a man most of the soldiers wanted to contend with. The former trapper was no giant, though he was a big man: Six-foot-two, one hundred eighty-five pounds, lean and hard, and he had a determined cast to his face.

Hudson didn't care what the soldiers thought of

him; he just plowed ahead until he was standing at the table, directly across from Bent. "Ho/a, amigo" he said. His deep, scratchy voice irritated the soldiers even more.

"Linus," Bent said with a note of relief in his voice. "Good to see you again."

"Good to be back." Without pausing, he asked bluntly, "What the hell's goin' on here, Bill?"

"The army's come to pay us a visit," Bent said drolly.

"I can see that. Why?"

"War's been declared on Mexico," one of the officers said. "We're using this dunghill as a staging area before we move on into Mexico."

Hudson turned his head and glared at the man. "What's your name, boy?" he asked harshly.

"Lieutenant Johan Bruckner," the officer said, drawing himself up proudly. He was not about to be intimidated by this wild-looking creature. He did, however, take stock of Hudson. The first thing he noted was the cold, determined gray eyes, and then the long, unkempt sandy hair. Hudson wore a filthy, tattered calico shirt, fringed buckskin pants, moccasins, and a wide-brimmed light-brown hat with a short, round crown. The edge of the rim was stitched with red yarn, and the hat had a band of red, white, and green beads with a weasel tail dangling off the back.

Bruckner figured Hudson's size and appearance were worrisome enough, but his armaments created even more concern. Hudson had two Colt Paterson revolving pistols stuck into the wide leather belt, barrels mostly frontward; an elkhorn-handled bowie knife with a wide, twelve-inch-long blade rested in a hard-leather sheath at the small of his back, and a tomahawk was stuffed in the belt just above the right buttock. Bruckner had seen that when Hudson had bulled his way through the crowd. The .50-caliber percussion Hawken rifle completed the fierce-looking creature's ensemble.

"Well, Lieutenant Johan Bruckner," Hudson said in a quiet rasp, "don't you and these other shit sticks with you have somethin' better to do than bother Mister Bent?"

"That's none of your concern," Bruckner said stiffly. He was the son of Prussian parents and though he had lived in America most of his life, he carried that heritage with him at all times.

"Like hell. You shits cain't even give my amigo here room enough to fart. Now why don't you and all the rest of your companeros go find somethin' to do."

"I won't have the likes of you telling me what to do," Bruckner said with no hint of an accent. There was more than a touch of insult and anger, though. And he seemed to be ready to challenge Hudson.

"Forget him, Johan," another officer said. "He's not worth arguing with. Hell, he looks like a damn savage. Probably acts like one, too." He chuckled a little, and his friends joined in.

Hudson stood stone faced as the soldiers drifted toward the door. Bruckner was the last to go and gave Hudson a dark, forbidding look. Hudson was not impressed.

When the officers were gone, Hudson turned and sat.

Bent looked at him and grinned lopsidedly. "I am obliged for you comin' to my 'rescue,' amigo," he said with a little laugh. The lines of tenseness Hudson had seen on Bent's face eased a little.

Hudson nodded. "Now, ol' hoss," he said quietly, "tell me just what the hell's goin' on here."

Bent waited until a large-around black woman set a tin mug in front of Hudson and a pot of coffee and plate of tamales in the center of the table.

CHAPTER 2

"Like that peckerwood Bruckner said, war's been declared on Mexico," Bent said after a sip of coffee.

Hudson had not hesitated; he had simply grabbed two tamales in one big, hard-knuckled hand and started chawing them down. "What in hell for?" he asked once he had swallowed.

"Be damned if I know," Bent said heatedly. "All I do know is that some asshole named Colonel Stephen Watts Kearny showed up here with regular army troops, plus a pisspot full of Missouri volunteers. There's damn near two thousand soldiers camped for miles up and down the Arkansas. And damn near every one of 'em's been a pain in my ass."

"I noticed," Hudson said dryly. "Why here, though?"

"Kearny's made the fort his headquarters or somethin'. Like Bruckner said, this is the stagin' area. Soon's they work up their courage, they're going to head down and try'n take over Santa Fe and Taos."

"That ought to be interestin'."

Bent shrugged. "A lot of the American boys down that way have been agitatin' for it. 'Specially since Texas became a state last year. I suppose many of 'em's thinkin' the same can be done with this part of Mexico." Bent sighed and sipped some coffee. "Trouble is, in the meantime, every goddamn officer Kearny's got with him seems to be in the fort—and more often than not in this room— every minute of the day."

"Send 'em on their way," Hudson said evenly.

"Wish I could, but you can't talk to them damn fools. I've talked to Kearny about it, but he don't much seem interested in makin' my life any easier. A few of the officers have stayed away unless they need to be here, for the most part, but not many."

Hudson stared at his friend for a few moments, then said more than asked, "There's more to it than jist some damn fool officers gettin' in your way, ain't there?"

Bent nodded. "Bastard's have took damn near every piece of horse and mule flesh I had here, plus all my supplies. I ain't got shit left here in the fort. My traders come back lookin' for new supplies, they're gonna be shit up a creek. Kearny and his quartermaster even had the goddamn gall to tell me the government'd pay for it all."

"You don't think they will?"

"Sure they will. The question is when. Christ, I hate dealin' with the government on such doin's. They're slower'n a cat coverin' shit on a flat rock. I might not see any of that goddamn money for two, three years."

"That don't shine."

"Hell, no, it don't."

Hudson shrugged. He felt sorry for his friend but he figured it was none of his concern. He was at best only semi patriotic, especially when it came to the military. Then he had a sudden thought. "Shit," he muttered, then asked, "You said the army took all your horses and mules."

"Yep," Bent said flatly.

"Damn, then that's why Pedro told me to take my animals and get the hell out of here, ain't it?"

"I expect it was," Bent said thoughtfully. "He knew what was goin' on." He paused. "But I don't think Kearny'll be interested in your saddle horse and a pack mule."

"Shit," Hudson snorted, "I got me ten goddamn prime Californy horses, boy. Plumb prime."

"Where'd you get 'em?" Bent asked though he knew. Linus Hudson wasn't the first former mountain man to turn his eyes toward California with the idea of stealing Mexican horses and selling them back here somewhere.

"Californy itself. Me, Joe Walker, and Peg Leg went out there a little while back with the purpose of relievin' some of them Californy haciendados of their horses. Took Mad Buffler and Whirlin' Storm with me."

"Where are they?"

"Headin' back toward their village. They saw the soldiers and figured they must've ridden through some of the Cheyenne camps. They wanted to get back and see if their families were all right."

"A reasonable thing for a man to think when he sees this shit here." He drained his coffee mug. "You bring them ponies here to sell 'em to me?" Most of the former mountain men did. Bent asked no questions about where the animals had come from, and he paid a fair price.

"Yep," Hudson said flatly. "But I think now that'd be plumb goddamn foolish." Hudson pushed to his feet. "I'd best go get 'em and head out. I'll be back to sell 'em to you once the army's gone—if I ain't sold 'em in Taos or somewhere."

"Hell, sit down, Linus," Bent said. He grinned ruefully up at Hudson. "I'll wager you them ponies're gone already."

"We'll jist see about that, goddammit," Hudson snapped.

"Hell, Linus, that'd be like pissin' into the wind. It might shine whilst it's comin' out but you ain't gonna take to it when it comes back and slaps you in the face."

"I'll git them ponies back," Hudson said tightly.

"Buffler shit. Now set yourself and eat some more."

Hudson sat, face hard with anger. "Hell, Bill, such doin's don't shine with this ol' boy. Damn, I spent three, four months on the trail bringin' them ponies back. It's about all I got that's worth anything."

"I expect it was." Bent paused and thought a moment. "Tell you what, buckin' the army ain't gonna get you nowhere but stuck in chains. I'll add your ponies to the bill I send the government."

"That's mighty generous of you, Bill," Hudson

said honestly. "But like you said, it might be some years before we see any of that money. I got to have some cash now."

Bent nodded. "You can work here for a spell."

"At the wages you pay?" Hudson snorted. "Damn, I'll be a hunnert years old before I get enough of a stake to move on."

Bent laughed. "You'll get paid better here than you will down in Taos, you crotchety old son of a bitch, and you know it." He paused again. "If you're real hardpressed and need to move on, I can probably advance you a bit of specie or supplies against your ponies."

"I jist might take you up on that, Bill," Hudson said, only a little mollified. "Let me think on it a bit." He stood again and grinned a little. "But I still got to see for myself if them ponies're gone. If they are, I'll be back here directly. If they're there, I'm pushin' on, and pronto."

"I'm still open for a wager," Bent said with a grin.

"Shit," Hudson snorted as he walked toward the door. He wasn't that foolish.

Hudson returned in just a few minutes and Bent could tell what had happened by the look on Hudson's face. "Told you, boy," Bent said quietly as Hudson took his seat.

"Piss off," Hudson snapped. Then he calmed himself a little. It would do him no good to turn nasty on his friend, who was in a far worse predicament than he was. "Ah, hell, Bill, I didn't mean that." It was about as close to an apology as he would give.

"I know."

"Christ, they even took my saddle horse and goddamn mule." Hudson sat, stewing some. "I tell you one thing, though, amigo," he finally said, still angry, "the army's gonna pay for these doin's, and pay big."

"You just mind when and where you take your revenge, ol' hoss. There's a heap of them blue coats out there."

Hudson nodded.

The two men sat there for a while, talking or not as they felt like it. They sipped coffee and ate almost constantly, as Charlotte, the black slave woman, shuttled out plates of this and that. Finally, though, Bent stood. "I best get some work done," he said, "while I still got the chance. I ain't often left alone these days."

"Should've said somethin' before, amigo" Hudson said. "I'd have moseyed on."

"Hell, it ain't friends like you that's the problem. It shined with me to set and jaw with you a spell." He headed off, back straight, head high.

Hudson sat there a little longer, but with each passing minute, he grew more and more angry at the army for having taken his animals. He was determined, though, to get his saddle horse and his mule back, come what may. It would take stealth, slyness, and determination, but he hadn't lived more than twenty years in the mountains and on the plains just by his good looks. Being a former mountain man, Hudson had faced nearabout every kind of danger and adversity the West could throw at him and he had survived it all. The army would never even know he was there, and they would never even miss his two animals.

The main problem, he figured, would be in finding his horse. With this many soldiers, plus wagons and such, there would have to be a couple thousand horses in these parts. They'd be spread out all over hell and creation, too, as the men tried to find enough grass to sustain the animals. It would take time but Hudson had nothing better to do. He would persevere.

He considered going to get Mad Buffalo and Whirling Storm to help him. The three of them could find the horse more quickly. They could also run off a heap of the army's confiscated stock, causing a plenty of confusion and annoyance. That thought was pleasing to Hudson but then he opted against it all. The army commanders might get so enraged that they would move in numbers against the Cheyennes. No, his thirst for revenge could not be stacked up against the possible loss of dozens of Cheyenne lives. He would have to do this himself.

Finally, he left the dining room, nodding his thanks to Charlotte and giving her a small coin for her service. He stepped outside. It was almost dark, but the heat was still oppressive. Things had calmed down in the placita somewhat. He tamped his pipe full of tobacco and lit it with a torch that he pulled out of its socket on a rafter.

Carrying an evergrowing grudge against the army, Hudson headed for the small saloon and billiards room that sat in isolated splendor on the second-floor walkway over the entrance to the stables out back. He figured he would try to drown his anger with liquor while trying to figure out how he would get to Mad Buffalo's village to see his wife, Stolen Back Woman.

The latter goal was becoming more and more pressing. He had not seen her since leaving for California. It didn't take him long to decide that he would steal an army horse—the first one he could find if he couldn't spot his own quickly—and would do it tonight. If he didn't get too drunk. He had enough sense to know better than to try such doin's while drunk. If that became a problem tonight, as it seemed too likely it would, he would plan it for tomorrow night.

That settled in his mind, Hudson got down to some serious drinking, feeding his anger at the army. He was doing quite a good job when, about two hours later, Lieutenant Johan Bruckner entered the saloon.

"There you are," Bruckner said with false good cheer. "I've been looking all over for you."

Hudson paid the haughty officer no mind since he didn't think Bruckner was talking to him. He was a little surprised when the pompous lieutenant plopped himself alongside Hudson at the small bar.

"I said I've been looking all over for you," Bruckner said, looking as if his dignity had been injured.

"You found me, dingleberry," Hudson growled. "Speak your piece and then get your festerin' carcass away from me."

"You shouldn't speak like that to me," Bruckner said stiffly.

"I'll speak to you any goddamn way I please, shit

stick. Now get on with it."

"You insufferable . . ." He paused when he got another look at those hard gray eyes. He straightened and then sneered a little. "Your animals have been conscripted to serve with the Army of the West," he said and held out a paper. "This is a government voucher that will be, I should think, more than equal compensation for those bony nags."

"They ain't nags, boy," Hudson said evenly. "They was prime blooded Spanish mounts straight from Californy."

"If you say so," Bruckner commented easily. He was beginning to enjoy taking Hudson down a peg or two. "Be that as it may, this is still a more than generous offer."

Hudson glanced at the paper. "Such an insultin' offer don't shine with this ol' hoss, you clapridden shit stick."

"I've had more than enough of your insolence," Bruckner said stiffly, angrily. "You damned savage half-breeds, or whatever the hell you are, are a blight on the good name of this country." Being an officer with more arrogance than brains, Bruckner continued insulting Hudson.

After a few minutes, some of the other officers began sniggering and chuckling as the unkind words piled up.

Hudson put up with it for a while. He was generally an even-tempered man. But twenty-one years in the mountains had hardened him, physically and socially, and he was not about to stand there and take guff from some damn fool, officer or not.

Without warning, he suddenly half spun and leveled Bruckner with one hard punch.

Bruckner's head hit the wall and he slid down the adobe until he was sitting on the floor looking dazed.

Five other junior officers leaped on Hudson, flailing away at the former trapper, and found that they had gotten ahold of a two-legged wildcat. Hudson was lean and hard, and he did not fight for fun. Within minutes, all five officers were down. Two of them were heavily injured after Hudson had tossed them out of the barroom door and down to the ground twenty feet below.

Hudson stood in the center of the room for a few moments, waiting to see if anyone else wanted to attack him. But the officers who remained in the saloon seem quite disinclined to challenge him. He nodded, turned, and headed for Bruckner.

The lieutenant was standing, though he wobbled considerably, and looked as if he couldn't focus his eyes.

Hudson grabbed him by the front of his blue blouse and jerked him forward. Without a word, he spun and shoved Bruckner. The officer stumbled but managed to keep upright. Hudson pushed him again, and Bruckner ended up in the doorway.

"Adios, dingleberry," Hudson said softly. Then he pounded Bruckner in the face.

The officer stumbled backward and then disappeared as he fell off the walkway. A moment later there was a thud.

Hudson turned and headed back into the saloon, taking up the spot where he had been before.

CHAPTER 3

Hudson stepped outside of the small, second-story saloon and billiards room and someone clubbed him on the side of the head, just behind the left ear. As he fell, he heard Bent's voice: "One of your men hits him again, Cap'n, and I'll shoot him—or you."

Hudson pushed himself up and shook his head, ignoring his rifle, which had fallen. He saw Bent holding a cocked, single-shot percussion pistol aimed at a middle-aged army captain. Hudson glared at the officer. "You know, boy," he growled, "such shit don't shine with this ol' boy."

"I'm Captain Denton Warfield, and you, sir, are under arrest," the officer responded, unfazed.

"That a fact?" Hudson asked sarcastically. He was sick of these soldiers and about ready to have another go-round with them, consequences be damned.

"Yes, sir, indeed it is," Warfield said calmly. Seeing the wild look in Hudson's eyes, he added, "I suggest you come along peacefully, Mister Hudson, lest one of my men gets nervous and fires at you."

"Best listen to him, Linus," Bent said flatly. He had uncocked his pistol and shoved it back into his belt. The situation grated on him, but there was little he could do to change it. About all he could do was try to see that Hudson got a fair shake. That was going to take some doing in and of itself.

"The hell I will," Hudson snarled. "It don't shine with me to be clubbed over the head."

"And it doesn't 'shine,' as you say, with the army to have several of its officers beaten and thrown from the parapet," Warfield noted coolly.

"Wasn't me who started them doin's, boy," Hudson said in equally cold tones. "It was them boys."

"That doesn't matter. The army frowns on such things."

"Then the army ought to teach its officers not to be so goddamn stupid. Then they wouldn't get the shit knocked out of 'em by some ol' critter who just wants to be left to his own self."

Warfield shrugged again. "Just who started it is up to a military court to decide," he said. He paused to let that sink in. "Now, will you submit peacefully or should I have my men take you by force?"

"Your boys'll be up to their asses in trouble, boy," Hudson said flatly. He tensed, ready for action.

"Go with them, Linus," Bent said quietly but urgently.

"Such don't shine with me, Bill," Hudson said simply.

"I know that, boy. Certain I do. But you resist, and all you're gonna do is get your ass put under."

"Shit, Bill," Hudson snorted, "the way numb nuts

here is talkin', I figure the army's fixin' to hang me anyway. That don't shine with me neither. I'd as soon go out fightin', and take a few of these fractious bastards with me."

"Hell, the army ain't gonna hang you just for bustin' up a few of its officers. And even if they are, if you're still alive, I might be able to get you out of this predicament. I'll do whatever I can for you when the army convenes the court. You know that."

Hudson pondered that for a few moments, then shrugged. "Reckon it would go some easier on me if I didn't go puttin' under any of these shit sticks."

"Chickenshit," one of the enlisted men muttered.

Hudson whirled and popped a soldier in the nose. He wasn't certain it was the one who had made the remark, but then again, he really didn't care all that much whether he hit the right one.

The soldier was surprised—and hurt—by the blow, and he dropped his rifle when his head bounced off the saloon wall.

Hudson turned back to face Warfield. "I see you don't teach anyone much in the army," he said sarcastically.

"Private Corbin will pay for his remark, Mister Hudson," Warfield said evenly. "Now, sir, shall we go?"

"Reckon you and your boys're gonna be a pain in my ass till I do, ain't you?"

"Yes, sir."

Hudson sighed. He eased out his Colt Patersons and held them toward Warfield. A sergeant stepped forward to take them.

"The knife and tomahawk, too," Warfield ordered.

Hudson handed them to the sergeant, too.

"Move," Warfield commanded, pointing to the stairs at the corner.

"Where to?"

"Mister Bent has kindly offered the use of one of the rooms below as a temporary guardhouse. While the door won't be locked, there will be two armed guards—and more, if necessary—just outside at all times. If you take so much as one step outside without permission, they have orders to shoot you down. Is that understood?"

Hudson could see no reason to answer beyond giving one curt nod. Then he turned and walked off, the soldiers falling in behind him.

As Hudson had known it would be, the storeroom in which he was placed was small and dark. It was lit only by two sputtering candles in sconces on the wall. The room was furnished only with a cot, a small table that looked more like a stool, and a half-full water bucket with a wooden ladle in it. Much of the room was taken up by bales of furs and boxes and barrels of trade goods. It left him little room to move around in.

When the soldiers left, Hudson stretched out on the cot. His head throbbed some from when he was clubbed, but it wasn't too bad. The whiskey he had consumed didn't help matters much. Since there was nothing else for him to do, he figured he'd nap a while. Or sleep, seeing as how it was nighttime. He had no need to check the room. It was simply one of Bent's ground-floor storerooms and Hudson knew Bent had put the minimal furnishings in just for him.

Hudson saw the outside of the room only four times over the next two days—when six armed men would escort him to the outhouse and then once around the placita. He was fed a bowl of atole in the morning and one in the afternoon. The cornmeal porridge was accompanied by a glass of warm cow's milk and was made palatable only by the sparse pieces of buffalo meat Bent had made sure Black Charlotte had slipped in it.

The rest of the time, Hudson sat in the dimly lit cell, bored. The boredom was the worst part for him. He was a man used to activity, not festering alone in a dank hole. He needed—craved—action. The tediousness of the situation ate steadily at his normally limited patience until he was in a sullen, rancorous humor.

Then Bent showed up with a battered Lieutenant Johan Bruckner and four armed guards. Through the open door, Hudson could see four more armed men waiting out in the shade of the portico.

"How's doin's, Linus?" Bent asked almost jovially.

"How the hell you think, boy?" Hudson growled in response. "I been settin' here on my ass for two days with nothin' to occupy my time and nothin' to fill my goddamn meatbag."

"You've been fed regular," Bent said, trying not to sound too sarcastic in front of Bruckner, who didn't look too bad, considering the pounding he took just over two days ago.

"Hell, you call two bowls of atole and a glass of

goddamn milk bein' fed? Shit," he added, drawing the word out. "I ain't even got no 'baccy for chrissakes."

"It's no worse than you deserve," Bruckner said almost smugly. He would've been self satisfied was it not for his mission here.

Bent gave the officer a sour look, then pulled a twist of tobacco from his belt pouch and tossed it to his friend.

Hudson caught it, and pointedly sliced off a hunk with a folding knife he kept in his own belt pouch. He put the knife and rest of the tobacco in his sack. Then he started chawing, and he sat. "So, Bill," he said, "what brings you and shit stick over there to my humble quarters?"

"We have a way to get you out of here," Bent said.

"That'd shine," Hudson said honestly.

"Several of the lieutenant here's troops disobeyed orders and crossed the river. They said they were goin' huntin'."

"You don't believe that, do you?" Hudson asked, looking hard at Bent.

The fort owner pulled up the tablestool and sat on it close to where Hudson perched on the edge of the cot. "Nope. But the reason they were over there ain't important right now. What is important is that three of them were took captive."

"How do you know they just didn't desert?" Hudson asked.

"Two others escaped and reported back to me," Bruckner responded flatly.

"They could be lyin'."

"One carried an arrow in his back."

"Comanche, of course," Bent said. "I expect they were on their way here to trade, spotted those damn fool soldiers and took after them."

"Think they're still alive?"

Bent shrugged. "Hell, you know them critters as well as I do. Ain't no tellin' what they'll do. Maybe keep 'em alive and try'n ransom 'em here later. Maybe sport with 'em some. Maybe killed 'em right off."

"What's all this got to do with me?" Hudson asked, knowing what was coming but wanting it out in the open.

"Army wants you to find 'em and bring 'em back," Bent answered. He found this almost amusing, seeing as how the army had caused him so much trouble.

"And I suppose you don't favor this, do you?" Hudson asked, fixing Bruckner with a hard glare.

"No," Bruckner growled. "But Colonel Kearny believes the Mexicans are massing troops between here and Santa Fe. We expect a hell of a fight and the general would like to have all the troops at his disposal that he can."

"That's bullshit," Hudson snapped.

Bruckner looked sour at having his white lie so easily unmasked. "Mainly, we just can't let these savages get away with such a thing—snatching men right out from under our noses. We must show them that such things are verboten." He sighed. "If we weren't at war with Mexico, we'd send out an entire regiment and run the savages to ground. But, since we are at war..."

Hudson thought that made some sense but it

still didn't ring true to him somehow. "Why me?" he asked.

"Only one here we can spare—or trust," Bent said. "Anyone else I could put my faith in is down in Mexico or out tradin' somewhere. Besides, you know more of this damned country than near anyone but me, Charlie or Kit."

Though he figured it might be the only way he was going to get out of his predicament, Hudson didn't like the idea. Something still bothered him about it all. He shook his head. "I ain't in the business of chasin' lost soldiers," he said flatly.

"They're not lost," Bruckner huffed. "They've been captured by savages."

Hudson shrugged. "They hadn't disobeyed orders—though considerin' who gave 'em, I can see why they did—they wouldn't've been caught up by them Comanches."

"We must get them back," Bruckner snapped. "We cannot let... "

"Cork it, Lieutenant," Bent said evenly, though with a harshness to his voice that was unmistakable. Bent looked at Hudson. "There's more to this than has been said," Bent remarked. He paused, sighed and then pushed on. "Those boys crossed the river because they were lookin' for some fun."

Hudson's eyebrows raised in question.

"They spirited off three of the Mexican women. Wives of my workers. They figured to sport with 'em over there, out of view of the fort—and their commander."

"And the women was caught up by the Comanches,

too?" Hudson queried.

Bent nodded. "I don't much give a shit about those blue coats," he said harshly, "but I'd sure as hell like to get them women back before they're abused too much."

Hudson glared up at Bruckner. "You aimin' to punish those boys if I get 'em back here?"

"For disobeying orders, yes," Bruckner answered without blinking.

"But not for takin' the women?"

"Of course not," Bruckner said indignantly.

"They're only Mexicans and everyone knows about Mexican women."

"They do, do they? And just what do they know about Mexican women?"

"That they are women of loose morals, with no concept of sinful ways in the eyes of God."

Hudson was about to spout off and tell Bruckner just what he thought of him, but he knew that it would do no good. Bruckner saw the world in only one way—his own. He would never be able to change.

Hudson still didn't like it, but he knew Bent was honest in his desire to have the women back. Now, it was not so much a matter of helping the army as it was of helping a friend. He finally nodded then looked at Bruckner. "I'll do it, but I want all my horses returned." He figured he had some leverage over the army now.

"The army needs those horses, Mister Hudson," Bruckner said in a withering tone.

"So do I."

"You were just going to sell them to Mister Bent."

Hudson shrugged. "That's my account."

Bruckner shook his head adamantly. "No, but I will return your saddle horse and your pack mule."

"You want those men of yours back, boy?" Hudson asked harshly. "If they're alive that is."

"That's what this is all about, Mister Hudson," Bruckner said, his tone sounding as if he thought Hudson had lost all his reason.

"And just how do you expect them to get back here? Walk from wherever the hell the Comanches have drug 'em off to?"

"You'll get three extra horses," Bruckner said flatly, feeling like a fool.

"Six," Bent said. "I want those women back as much as you want your goddamn blue coats back. They'll need horses, too."

Swallowing his pride—after all, Colonel Kearny had ordered him to have someone track down the captured men—Bruckner nodded.

"I'll need supplies," Hudson said.

"The army has none to spare," Bruckner said, feeling as if he were getting back a little at Hudson. "You'll have to get them elsewhere."

Bent rolled his eyes and muttered, "Asshole." He sighed. "I'll supply you, Linus."

Hudson nodded and then looked at Bruckner. "Just one more thing before I agree to this goddamn foolishness, boy. I want all the horseshit charges against me for that little fandango the other night done away with. And not reinstated," he added after a moment.

Bruckner nodded, angry. He had been told that

offering that would be an option for him. He had not planned to do so, though. It irked him that Hudson had brought it up. He could do nothing but acquiesce.

"Good," Hudson said. He waved a hand at the soldiers standing by. "Now, send your boys away so's I can start gettin' ready."

"You'll leave as soon as possible?" Bruckner hinted.

"You in a hurry?" Hudson countered.

Bruckner nodded. "Colonel Kearny plans to leave Bent's Fort around the end of July," he said. "He would like the captured men back by then. That gives you only three weeks or so."

"I cain't promise you nothin', boy," Hudson said. "Them Comanches move fast and far."

"Do what you can, Mister Hudson." He paused and then grinned slyly. "Oh, and I almost forgot to tell you. I'll be sending a patrol with you."

Hudson was set to argue, but Bent's look and the knowledge that he had little choice kept him quiet. He simply nodded.

CHAPTER 4

Within an hour, Hudson rode out of the adobe fort with seven mounted Dragoons behind him. To the soldiers' surprise, he headed east, winding through the strung-out army camps along the Arkansas, instead of crossing the river near the fort.

Sergeant Alfred Lowell, who was in charge of the Dragoon detail, wondered about it for a while, but said nothing. Until Hudson turned north a few miles east of the fort. At that point, Lowell rode up alongside Hudson. "I thought we was supposed to head south across the river, Mister Hudson," he said. "Now, I ain't maybe the best man in the world with compass directions, but this sure as hell seems to be north the way we're goin' now."

"It is."

"But why?"

Hudson shrugged. "I got some little business to tend to up this way before we head down into Comanche country."

Lowell was not happy with that, but Lieutenant

Bruckner had told him that Hudson was the scout and guide and that he should be listened to—unless or until Hudson seemed to go too far with something.

Several hours later, Lowell spotted an Indian village in the near distance. He quickly trotted up alongside Hudson again. "We goin' there?" he asked, pointing.

"Yep."

"Why?" Lowell was more than a little concerned.

"Told you. I got business to see to."

"I ain't so sure about this, Mister Hudson."

"You don't have no say in it, boy," Hudson replied. He was still angry at the army in general, and of no mood to be polite to anyone wearing a uniform.

Lowell had figured as much, but that did not lessen his worry any. "Just what kind of Indians are they?" he finally asked.

"Cheyennes. Southern branch," Hudson answered after looking at Lowell a moment to see if the sergeant was aiming to be disrespectful. He decided Lowell wasn't.

"What's your business here, Mister Hudson?" Lowell asked, polite and curious. "If you don't mind my askin'."

"Important doin's, boy," Hudson said evenly. Then he grinned. "I ain't seen my wife in a dog's age, boy," he said, "and I plan to have at least one night with her before headin' out again."

"You're married to an Indian woman?" Lowell asked, a note of condescension in his voice.

"Yep. You got a problem with that, boy?"

Lowell thought about that for a few minutes,

then shook his head. "No, sir, can't say as I really do. Just seemed strange at first is all." He paused and looked at Hudson in question. "Why an Indian woman, though, Mister Hudson? Again, if you don't mind me askin'."

Hudson shrugged. "There's jist somethin' about an Injin woman's ways, boy."

"They pretty free with their favors—as I've heard?" Lowell asked. "Meanin' no disrespect, sir," he hastily added.

Hudson laughed. "Hell, yes. But they ask a heap of foofaraw for it." He paused and grew serious. "But that ain't no reason to marry one, boy. You can sport with a plenty of 'em, but when it comes to marryin' 'em, that's another thing. Still, they shine in those doin's, too. They're hard workers. Not like them white women you meet back in the settlements, always wantin' things done for 'em. Hardly ever wantin' you to sport with 'em and such. Injin women're warm and carin'. They ain't subject to women's ills like so many white women. They're a hell of a lot more adventuresome, too, in the robes and out of 'em." He laughed again.

"You make 'em sound mighty special, Mister Hudson."

"You don't believe me, Sergeant?" Hudson asked in not unfriendly tones. He had decided that perhaps Sergeant Alfred Lowell might not be all that bad a fellow despite his being a soldier.

"Not to say that I don't believe you, Mister Hudson. It's just that I. . ." He paused, chewing his mustache as he thought. "Well," he finally added, "let's just say

I got a few doubts, considerin' the only Injin women I've ever seen were them poor devils out by Fort Leavenworth and such."

"Shit, boy, them ain't Injins no more. You jist wait till you see these Cheyennes. Now those are some shinin' Injins. Waugh, damn if they ain't. Purty women, fearsome warriors."

The last brought back to Lowell just where they were heading. "Those Cheyennes gonna accept me and the rest of the boys, us bein' part of the army and all?" he asked nervously.

"I expect they will, but you nary can tell," Hudson said with a twinkle in his eyes.

Lowell did not see the twinkle and it was with severe discomfort that he and his men rode into the Cheyenne village.

A woman bolted out of the lodge where Hudson had stopped and dismounted. Hudson spun and scooped her up in his arms and hugged her with an aggressive lovingness.

"Your wife, I take it?" Lowell questioned dryly despite his nervousness at being in the village.

"Yep. Her name's Stolen Back Woman." Hudson turned as Mad Buffalo and Whirling Storm strode up and the three greeted each other. They spoke in Cheyenne for some moments, then Hudson looked at the soldiers. "You boys're on your own," he said. "This here is Mad Buffler," he added, pointing to that warrior, "and this is Whirlin' Storm." He pointed again. "They speak passable English and they'll show you around and watch over you some. You're free to go where you will in the village, except in the lodges, unless you're invited. If you got some foofaraw you can afford to get rid of, you might spark a deal with one of the women for a roll in the robes. They turn you down, though, you leave 'em be."

"What about our horses?" Lowell asked.

"Mad Buffler's and Whirlin' Storm's nephews'll take care of 'em."

"They gonna do a good job of it?"

"They get a heap better care here than they would if their tendin' was left to soldiers." He paused. "Jist remember to respect these people and their ways. You do that, and they'll respect you." He grinned. "Now I got business to tend to. Adios."

Fear growing, the soldiers handed over their horses to a number of boys, all of whom seemed to be in the vicinity of ten years old. Then they followed Mad Buffalo and Whirling Storm as the two Cheyennes began taking them around the village.

The seven soldiers drew a considerable amount of attention from the Cheyennes. Most of it, though, did not seem hateful, just interested. Lowell's curiosity grew as he and his men walked around. Everything fascinated him. As Hudson had told him, the Cheyennes were uniformly tall and handsome. The men looked fierce, though generally friendly. Lowell decided he would not want to have to go to war against them, however. The women were comely and open. Several smiled at him or his men, as if in invitation.

Lowell mentioned that to Mad Buffalo, then asked, "Are they really interested in us? Or are they just bein' friendly?"

"Maybe they're interested," Mad Buffalo responded with a grin, his broad, fleshy nose wrinkling up with the action. "Probably 'cause of Fierce Bear."

"Who?" Lowell asked, mouth dry.

"Fierce Bear. It's the People's name for Linus. I think them women think all white men're as good as Fierce Bear."

"Why would they think that?"

"Like all good Cheyenne women, Stolen Back Woman talks to the others," Whirling Storm said with a laugh. "They tell every other woman about how we are as men."

"We'd probably disappoint 'em somethin' awful," Lowell said in embarrassment.

Whirling Storm shrugged. "Maybe you'll get the chance."

Lowell nodded, but he hoped he did, embarrassment, disappointment, or not. He kept quiet about it, though, as he continued to follow the two Cheyennes around the village. He took in everything he saw, captivated by just about everything. Children, a good many of them entirely naked, ran around, screeching and playing. The youngsters would stop when they saw the white men in their blue uniforms and stare. But the novelty would wear off quickly and they would go back to their games, secure in their fearlessness.

Lowell checked weapons tripods outside lodges as closely as possible—after asking permission to do so—and questioned his two guides about the meat racks and games being played and the lodges themselves.

As the afternoon and evening progressed, the Dragoons began to relax, so much so that three of them, including Lowell, tried getting friendly with Cheyenne women. Lowell thought he would be repulsed by an Indian woman, but he was astounded to find Little Kettle's dusky skin tones, soft voice, and eagerness intoxicating.

Lowell didn't have much to give Little Kettle, though he wished to stay the night with her. After their first round of lovemaking, they lay there in each other's arms. Lowell was glad to see that Little Kettle did not seem inclined to have him leave. That was encouraging.

Things took a turn for the worse, though, when he heard a scream, and then another. He jumped up and scrambled into his pants and shirt and belt, then charged outside.

Hudson had heard the scream, too. Wearing only moccasins and a breechcloth and carrying a revolver, he bolted outside. He stopped, looking around, until he thought he spotted the source of the trouble. He ran.

He found one of the Dragoons—Private Gregg Farmer—looming over a young woman. He was reaching back to hit her again when Hudson plowed into him. They rolled several times, Hudson hanging on. When they stopped, Hudson jumped up. Grabbing Farmer by the hair, he flung him into a stunted tree along the creek. Farmer's back hit the tree and he groaned a little.

Hudson tossed aside the pistol. He fully intended to kill Farmer but he wanted to do it by hand. As

Hudson headed toward the soldier, three of Farmer's fellow Dragoons stepped between the two.

"That's far enough, Mister Hudson," Private Halsey Butterworth ordered nervously. He and his two companions were holding weapons on Hudson.

"Git the hell outta my way, boys, before you git hurt, too," Hudson growled.

"I can't let you do that, Mister Hudson," Lowell said, arriving to stand next to his men. He was puffing a little from the run.

Cheyennes had gathered around behind Hudson. They no longer looked friendly to Lowell.

"I don't kill him, the Cheyennes will," Hudson snapped. "And if they do it, it'll be neither pretty nor done too quickly."

"Then they'll have to kill us all," Lowell said flatly. "I can't let these Injins—or you—kill an American soldier."

An irate Red Hand—one of the principal chiefs of the village—stomped up to Hudson and barked at him in Cheyenne for a bit. Hudson responded in the same language. After a while, Hudson finally turned to Lowell. "You got any idears on this, boy?" he asked. "Red Hand here's about to kill him, you, me and all the rest of us white men."

Lowell thought about it for a spell, then said. "Tell the chief there that I—and the army—will see that Private Farmer'll be punished good and proper."

Hudson translated for Red Hand, then said to Lowell. "When?"

"Soon's we get back from this mission."

"That's no good," Hudson said after conversing in

harsh tones with Red Hand. "Red Hand's half froze to raise that shit stick's hair here and now."

"I can't allow that."

"You goddamn fool," Hudson snarled. "You're gonna git all of us kilt because that stupid bastard tried to abuse a woman. Hell, a girl. White Blanket ain't but thirteen."

"I give my word that he'll be punished."

"Your word don't mean shit to these people," Hudson hissed.

"Yours does," Lowell said evenly.

"I reckon it does. But it ain't going to much longer you keep on this way, boy. These people're madder'n all hell. Things like that dumb bastard tried don't sit well with the Cheyennes. They respect their women too goddamn much for such doin's. And there's gonna be blood shed—white man's blood—if you don't give him up."

Lowell shook his head. He was still afraid, but he was not showing it. And he was determined not to give in here.

Hudson fumed. "It don't shine with me to get rubbed out for the likes of him, boy."

The idea didn't set very well with Lowell either. He had never taken a liking to Farmer. But he could not just give over one of his soldiers to a village of Indians to torture. Still, he was beginning to really understand the seriousness of the situation and what Farmer's actions meant to the Cheyennes. He thought furiously, trying to come up with a compromise. Suddenly it came to him. "How's this, then, Mister Hudson?" he said. "What happens if I

THE FRONTIERSMAN | 43

punish him myself? Here and now."

"What're you fixin' to do to him?" Hudson countered, intrigued by the idea.

"I ain't sure. I might need your help in determining that. But he won't be killed. I must insist on that point."

Some of Hudson's anger disappeared. He nodded and turned to Red Hand. It took him plenty of talking—and a great reliance on the goodwill he had built up over the years with these people—but Hudson finally convinced the Cheyennes that allowing Lowell to punish the offender would be best.

Finally, he turned back to the soldiers. "Red Hand agrees, but the Cheyennes'll have to see the punishment for themselves."

Lowell nodded. "I accept." He paused, then asked, "But what're we gonna do to him?"

"I got an idea. Have a couple of your boys go and get a log. Maybe six-feet long and a foot or so around."

Lowell nodded again and gave the order. It was a tense fifteen minutes before the two men returned, carrying a log between them.

Under Hudson's direction, the soldiers placed the log across a protesting Farmer's shoulders and tied his hands around the top of it. Done, Hudson whispered to Lowell, who nodded and said, "Private Farmer, you will march the length of this village, back and forth, continuously through the night. You will be allowed to stop twice during the night to piss. Your punishment'll stop an hour before we are to leave in the morning so that you might get yourself ready."

"I ain't gonna do it, Sarge," Farmer protested. "No, sir."

"Oh, yes you goddamn will, Private," Lowell said harshly. "And you'll do it under the watchful eyes of several Cheyennes. They'll be happy to brain you should you give them a hard time. Now get your ass movin'.'"

As an angry, and somewhat bewildered Farmer trudged off, a phalanx of hooting, jeering Cheyennes following him, Lowell turned to Hudson. "This might not be all that appropriate considering the circumstances, Mister Hudson," he began.

"Ask it, boy. Nobody else'll do it for you."

"Well, me'n and Little Kettle were gettin' along right well before this ruckus started. I ain't so sure she was gonna let me stay the night with her, seein's how short of foofaraw I am, but I thought there might be a chance." He trailed off, embarrassed.

Hudson looked at Red Hand and explained. The old chief finally nodded and Little Kettle was brought forth. The question was broached to her. She smiled at Lowell and nodded happily. A moment later, the young Cheyenne woman and the tall, gangly sergeant were walking swiftly toward Little Kettle's lodge.

CHAPTER 5

Farmer was a sullen man in the morning as he sat at a fire with his fellow soldiers, except for Lowell. Only one of his comrades—Private Tommy McKagan—had any sympathy for him, however. The four others ignored him as they ate their meal. They were still a little fearful of the Cheyennes, worried that the Indians would not be satisfied with the punishment meted out to Farmer and so do something to them. It was much easier to deride Indians from afar when you were with thousands of other soldiers. But here, in the very camp of the savages, outnumbered by a great deal and knowing the Indians did not much like them, it was a very different story.

Sergeant Lowell drifted by his men's camp after a while, a smile of satisfaction stretched across his broad, square-jawed face. He noted Farmer's sullenness, which he expected, but he didn't think the soldier would cause him any trouble, at least not for a while.

"You have yourself a good el' time, Sarge?" Private

Elroy Hogg asked with a leering wink.

"Not that it's any of your concern, Private," Lowell answered evenly, "but since you asked, you're goddamn right I did." He could not help himself. His night with Little Kettle had been so wondrous that he felt a need almost to brag or at least crow a little.

"Tell us all about it, Sarge," Hogg urged. He was a small, wiry, generally disgusting man with a perpetual chip on his shoulder and a decided lack of manners of any kind.

"Hell, you boys're too young to hear such things," Lowell said, grinning to cover his annoyance at the impertinence of the question. "You boys seen Mister Hudson this morning?"

When all the soldiers but Farmer shook their heads, Lowell strode off. He thought he remembered which one of the two dozen or so lodges was Hudson's. He only hoped he was right. He would feel like an utter fool if he went calling at the wrong place.

Lowell also was considerably relieved as he walked through the village that the Cheyennes seemed to be friendly toward him once more. He had worried that they might carry some enmity for him, or for any soldier, after what Farmer had done last night.

He stopped at the lodge he thought was the correct one and said softly, "Mister Hudson? You in there?" He waited a few moments and then repeated his call.

The flap opened, and a young, pretty face emerged. Lowell recognized Stolen Back Woman right off. "Come in," she said.

"Thank you, ma'am," Lowell said as he stepped inside. He felt odd about using the term with a Cheyenne woman, but he thought it only polite and it seemed proper somehow. He stopped just inside and let his eyes adjust to the gloom for a few seconds. It was warm outside already, though it was barely after dawn. Inside the lodge, it was downright hot since the sides of the tipi had not been rolled up yet to let in the air.

Lowell spotted Hudson sitting at the far side of the fire, facing the entrance. Mad Buffalo and Whirling Storm were at the fire with him.

"Well, come and sit down, boy," Hudson said.

"I don't want to intrude," Lowell said lamely.

"You ain't intrudin'. Besides, me and my two amigos here were just discussin' somethin' that might interest you."

With a questioning look in his eyes, Lowell sat. He nodded thanks when Stolen Back Woman handed him a horn bowl of stewed buffalo and a tin cup of harsh, black coffee. He ate and sipped a little, then asked, "So what's the discussion?"

"Mad Buffler and Whirlin' Storm want to go with us," Hudson said evenly. He seemed a little amused to Lowell.

"Why?" Lowell asked, surprised.

"They think they might be able to help win release of them soldier boys without a fight."

"Is that possible?"

Hudson shrugged. "Might be. The Cheyennes and their allies, the Arapahos, used to be deadly enemies of the Comanches and Kiowas. But they all made peace about six years ago. Had themselves a big whooptedo a couple miles from the fort. Bill Bent helped set that up. Goddamn, you should've seen them doin's, boy. Christ, there was Injins as far as the eye could see in any direction. And more horses than a man could count. There was feastin' and yarnin' and all kinds of such doin's. Waugh! That was some now."

"Does this peace mean they no longer fight?" Lowell asked, trying to bring the subject back to the matter at hand.

"I wouldn't go so far as to say that," Hudson noted. "But they're on mostly friendly terms. Hell, they even go on war parties together these days. I'll tell you true, boy, that still amazes me."

"But will they be able to help us?" Lowell asked, growing somewhat exasperated.

"Who knows. Both of 'em's been to war with the Comanches, so those critters ought to listen to 'em, at least. Cain't hurt."

Lowell nodded, thinking. Suddenly realization hit him. "You're plannin' to take these two whether I like the idea or not, aren't you?" he questioned. That explained Hudson's almost amused look, he figured.

"Yep," Hudson answered without shame or gloating.

"I object," Lowell said, trying to be serious. Then he laughed. "At least my protest is official, in case any of those fractious officers back at the fort see fit to question me about it." He grew serious. "I must ask, though, Mister Hudson—can these two men be trusted?"

"I can trust 'em," Hudson said without hesitation.

Lowell didn't have to think about it long. "That's good enough for me," he said firmly. He went back to eating his stew and sipping coffee.

Stolen Back Woman came over to kneel beside her husband. She spoke briefly in his ear in Cheyenne. When Hudson answered in kind, she rose and went outside.

After she had left, Lowell asked, "Do you have any children, Mister Hudson?" He had been surprised not to see any in the lodge. Hudson didn't much seem like the fatherly type to him, but still, one had to figure that any man who had spent as much time with Indian women as Hudson did had to have at least some children. "If you don't mind my askin'," he added hastily. He was truly interested but he also was a man who was not comfortable prying into others' affairs.

"Got me three all told. Shinin', they are, every damn one 'em. Two of 'em's from my first Cheyenne wife, Speckled Pony. She's been gone near six years now." His tone held just a touch of wistfulness and loss. "One of 'em's a boy. He's nigh onto twelve, I reckon. The other's a girl. She's edgin' on ten summers. Me'n Stolen Back Woman got us a son, too, a hellraisin' four-year-old we call Black Hand."

"Where are they?" Lowell asked, interested. It seemed odd to him that the youngsters were not with their parents, even if two of the children had a different mother.

"All with aunts and uncles. Such is the Cheyenne way. Aunts and uncles teach 'em what they need to know."

"Don't you want to send them to school back east or somethin' to get a proper education?"

"Shit, boy, all they need to know they can learn right here with the People. Or from me later. Most of what's taught in them white schools ain't worth a shit, boy. Not that this chil' can see."

"But..." Lowell stopped before he got any more out. He knew it was useless to try to debate the point with Hudson. He also knew that it was none of his concern. "My apologies, Mister Hudson, for tryin' to stick my nose in business where it didn't belong," he said honestly.

"De nada." He was coming to like Lowell. The tall, red-faced sergeant wasn't like most soldiers Hudson had encountered. He seemed a lot more thoughtful. And reasonable. After a brief pause, Hudson said, "But now you best see that your boys're gittin' ready, Sergeant," Hudson said. "I aim to be pullin' out before long." After a night with Stolen Back Woman, Hudson had a somewhat better outlook on life, and he was eager to be on the move again.

Lowell nodded and rose. He headed for the outside, but then stopped and turned back. "Is there any chance I might get to see Little Kettle again—after we finish our mission, I mean?" he asked, embarrassed.

"Took a shine to that little gal, did you, Sergeant?" Hudson countered with a friendly grin.

"Yessir, and I don't mind admittin' to such."

"She's a fine one, Little Kettle is. I cain't say for sure, but I reckon she and her pa'll be open to such a thing."

"Obliged," Lowell said guiltily, then turned and left.

Soon after, Hudson and his two friends went outside. The Cheyennes headed off to get ready. Stolen Back Woman had Hudson's horse saddled and his mule packed. He nodded thanks and kissed her lightly. "I'll be back before long," he said in Cheyenne. "Don't you worry about me."

"I always worry when you're gone," Stolen Back Woman said simply.

"There's no need for that."

"Maybe not," she said in Cheyenne, shrugging. "But I can't help feeling that way. And I miss you, too."

"Now that's something I can understand, woman," Hudson said in Cheyenne. He laughed a little. "What woman wouldn't miss a handsome man like me?"

"Bah," Stolen Back Woman growled. But she chuckled.

Hudson pulled her close for a moment, then released her. "To tell the truth, I miss you an awful lot when I'm off on business."

Stolen Back Woman smiled, knowing her man was speaking the truth.

Hudson pulled himself into the saddle, fighting off the sudden urge to just stay here and tell the soldiers to find their own missing fellows. Being in Stolen Back Woman's company would be a hell of a lot more pleasing than traveling across the dust-laden desolation of the Llano Estacado in the company of seven soldiers. But he could not do that. He winked at Stolen Back Woman and then trotted toward the soldiers' little camp.

All the troops were ready, except Farmer. The private sat on a small log. He looked sore and exhausted, but the light of arrogance and rebellion still glittered in his deep-set eyes.

"Best move your ass, boy," Hudson said to Farmer. "We've got little time to waste."

"Eat shit, Hudson," Farmer snarled. He was in no mood to be dictated to by anyone, least of all a flea-bitten coot like Linus Hudson.

"Get up and movin', Private!" Lowell bellowed from across the soldiers' small camp.

"I ain't goin' no goddamn where, Sarge," Farmer said defiantly. "Not after I been run ragged all goddamn night cartin' that goddamn log. And all because of some goddamn squaw."

Lowell walked to Farmer and loomed over him. "You will get your ass up, Private Farmer, and you will move with haste," Lowell ordered, his voice filled with menace.

"Or what?" Farmer asked with a sneer. He squinted up at his sergeant, still defiant.

"Or ... ?" Lowell fumed. He was befuddled. Back at the encampment, punishment would be swift and certain. But out here, Lowell was not so sure. Oh, he was confident enough in his authority and he was more than certain he could take Farmer in a fight if it came to that. But such signs of insubordination had to be punished and there was no time to really deal with such things.

"Or, you dumb sack of shit," Hudson said evenly but harshly, taking the onus off Lowell, "we'll leave your sorry ass here. How would that suit you, numb nuts?"

"You ain't gonna do no goddamn such thing, you old windbag," Farmer said, still certain of himself.

Hudson almost smiled. "I'm leavin' soon's Whirlin' Storm and Mad Buffler get here, Sergeant Lowell," he said, grinning a little when he saw the look of annoyance on Farmer's face. "I expect you and your boys to come along. Shit stick there can set as long as he likes, though I doubt the People'll be real pleased about havin' him here."

"He'll be ready," Lowell said tightly. "Or he'll be left behind."

Less than five minutes later, the two Cheyenne warriors rode up. Mad Buffalo wore a buffalohorn headdress tied under his chin. He wore painted leggings and a buckskin breechcloth and moccasins. Whirling Storm was almost naked. He wore only a buckskin breechcloth and moccasins. Two eagle feathers were tied to his loosely flowing hair. Each man had a bow case and quiver slung across his back, a shield on his left arm, and a lance in hand. Their saddles were simply pads of buffalo fur, their reins a length of horsehair rope tied to the pony's lower jaw.

"Time," Hudson said. He turned his horse and began riding slowly out of the camp, with his two Cheyenne friends beside him. A moment later, Sergeant Alfred Lowell led five of his troopers after Hudson and the Indians. Two of the soldiers drove the extra horses and the pack mules ahead of them.

Sitting there, Private Gregg Farmer suddenly realized that Hudson, Lowell, and the others were indeed going to leave him. He glanced around at the unfriendly faces and shivered. He didn't fully understand why but it seemed to him that the Cheyennes hated him. It made no sense to him, but he had never thought that anything any Indian did made sense. He did, however, push himself up, trying to ignore the aches and tiredness. He saddled his horse in minutes, jumped on, and galloped after his companions, worried all the time that the Cheyennes would not allow him to leave the camp alive. He made it, though, and was soon trotting along with the other soldiers.

The day was already wickedly hot and dry when they left the village. It grew progressively worse as the day lengthened. The sky's blue was unbroken even by the faintest wisp of cloud and the sun pounded down on the barren, dusty land, and the men creeping across the landscape.

Several hours later, they were moving through the army camps again, working their way toward the river. Mad Buffalo and Whirling Storm rode proudly, their mien almost regal in their arrogance. Despite being surrounded by blue coats—most of whom watched them with condescension mixed with a dash of worry—they were unafraid.

Then they were in the river and swimming the horses across it. The water cooled them a little and washed some of the trail dust off them.

Hudson would not let them stop on the other side since they were still in view of the soldiers in their sprawling camp. Many of the troopers were lining the northern bank watching the small group. It wasn't so much that they were interested; it was more that this was the only thing that had broken the monotony since they had gotten to this godforsaken outpost.

CHAPTER 6

The small group moved at a good pace, heading south and east. Mad Buffalo and Whirling Storm were in advance of the others, one ahead toward the left flank, the other on the opposite side. Hudson and Lowell followed a little behind, with the horses and pack animals following them. The six troopers brought up the rear, herding the animals ahead of them.

"You know where to start lookin', Mister Hudson?" Lowell asked as they made their way along in the brutal heat.

Hudson waved a hand around at the vast emptiness through which they rode. There was nothing out there, as far as the eye could see. Just endless land, shimmering heat waves, sagebrush, short, browning grass, and the occasional small hump of a ridge.

"Not very helpful," Lowell said dryly.

"That's a certain fact, boy. This is Comanche land, Sergeant. As far as you can see and a far, far piece beyond. Much of it's called the Llano Estacado.

That's Spanish for Staked Plains. There's a shitload of empty out here. There's several main bands of Comanches, though they don't deal with each other much. Standoffish folks, they are, even amongst themselves, in many ways. They call everything from Taos and Santa Fe to the eastern settlements of Texas, from Mexico almost to the Platte River their land. They don't take kindly to trespassers, red or white. They've been known to ride more'n a thousand miles to raid. They move fast, they move silent when they want to, and they can live in lands that'd kill a white man easy."

"I've heard they're peaceable Indians," Lowell said.

"Where'd you hear that shit?" Hudson asked with a snort.

"The army sent a party of Dragoons down here several years ago to meet the Comanches and try to get them to make peace with the Pawnees and other tribes. From what I heard, that mission was successful. The Dragoons were treated well by the Comanches and everyone got along famously."

"Sure they did," Hudson agreed. "Till just as soon as the soldiers were out of sight again. Then they went straight back to their old ways. The Comanches might be savages, boy, but they ain't fools. They knew damn well what kind of trouble they could bring on themselves by treatin' them blue coats poorly. Besides, they're not really at war with the Americans. Their main enemy—amongst white men—is the Mexicans, even though they trade with them as often as not. They figure that if they treat the Americans nice, well, maybe the Americans just might leave 'em the hell alone so they can set their sights on the Mexicans."

Hudson stopped to put some tobacco in his mouth and begin working it into a decent consistency. He eventually leaned over and spat, then settled back into the saddle, satisfied. "Them Comanches is hard critters, boy, and don't you doubt it. They're meaner'n any people you'll ever meet. One thing you don't want to do, boy, is underestimate the fierceness and tenacity of the Comanches. They can do things to stay alive men like me'n you can't even think of."

Hudson paused. "Knowin' what I do about the Comanches, I don't hold out much hope of those friends of yours bein' alive. I didn't want to say anything about it back at the fort, though. I did, the army might've never let me out of my predicament."

"You think they were killed right off?" Lowell asked hopefully, ignoring, for the most part, Hudson's self-serving statement. He would've done the same in Hudson's position.

"Nope. I figure the Comanches raced back to their village fast as they could, sported with them women the blue coats stole and then used the soldier boys to amuse the people of the village for a while. Then—and only then—were they killed."

Hudson paused and looked at Lowell. He grinned grimly. "Unless, of course, they got to be too much of a pain in the ass. Then the Comanches would've killed 'em without a thought, peeled their hair, and went on their merry way."

"That's horrible," Lowell breathed, rather shocked. He had known—well, at least heard—that the western Indians did such things, but he was never really willing to totally believe it.

Hudson shrugged. "The Comanches don't shine with me at all, boy, but they're only doin' what they see is right in their lights."

"You agree with what they do?" Lowell asked. He was astounded at the very thought.

"Nope," Hudson said easily. "But I've seen as bad things and worse done by Americans. And Mexicans. And other Indians. Part of the troubles between white men and red are because of man's natural arrogance. Neither side can see he's jist as bad as the other when the chips're down."

"I ain't so sure I like the implications of that, Mister Hudson," Lowell said thoughtfully. "Maybe that's because I really don't want to accept the truth of it."

"Life ain't so easy out here, boy, if a man has any charitable or decent thoughts at all. Once you start tryin' to see Injins in a proper light, things get a mite confused, because then you got to look at yourself jist as hard. There's many a chil' cain't do that, Sergeant. It's easier for 'em to just not see Injins as human beings."

Lowell was not at all sure what to say to that, so he kept his silence, at least for a while. Though he had no proof of it, of course, he instinctively knew that Hudson was speaking the truth. He was uncomfortable with the thought of looking so deeply into himself.

They camped that night in a spot that seemed little different from any they had passed that long day. There were no trees for protection or for wood. Lowell could see no landmarks. More importantly, he did not see a source of water.

"You sure this is the right spot to spend the night, Mister Hudson?" he asked after explaining his reservations.

Hudson grinned. "You see any better place?"

Lowell looked around in the gathering dusk and then shook his head. "I have to think of my men, though," he said. "And the animals."

"You think me and the Cheyennes have survived out here all these years by not knowin' what we was doin'?"

"No, sir, I suppose hot."

"Jist relax, Sergeant. We'll be fine." He paused and then grinned again. "Leastways till we meet up with some Comanches."

"Not a very heartening thought," Lowell said seriously. He sighed. "Well, what do we use—if anything—for fires?"

"Ye never used buffler chips?" Hudson asked, surprised. He couldn't believe Lowell and the others had marched across the vast plains from Fort Leavenworth to Bent's Fort without having used buffalo chips for fires.

"Of course. I just wasn't sure there were any out here. I haven't seen any buffalo on this side of the river."

"They've just moseyed on north," Hudson said. "Have a couple of your men gather some before it gets dark. The rest can tend the horses. They best eat and hit their bedrolls, since I aim to be on the move early."

The temperature was pleasant as the group pulled out in the morning, shortly after daybreak, but it warmed up fast and showed little sign of easing off any time soon.

About an hour after leaving their small camp, Whirling Storm came racing back. He pulled up next to Hudson and spoke for a few moments in Cheyenne.

Hudson nodded and then looked at Lowell. "Whirlin' Storm and Mad Buffler found somethin' a couple miles out. Let's ride."

Following Whirling Storm, they soon arrived at where Mad Buffalo stood, his pony ground staked. Hudson stopped and slid out of the saddle. Tossing his reins to Private Helmut Hochner, Hudson walked swiftly to Mad Buffalo, who now knelt. Lowell was right behind the frontiersman.

"Bones," Lowell said stupidly.

Hudson squinted up at him in annoyance. Then he looked at Mad Buffalo. "How old?" he asked.

"A day. Maybe day and a half."

Hudson nodded, silently looking over the scattered bones.

"They from one of my men?" Lowell asked, voice tight.

"Nope," Hudson answered. He fingered a bit of cloth amidst the bones. "Dress material," he said. He touched a bit of silver with a forefinger. "Piece of a necklace," he added.

"One of Mister Bent's Mexicans?" Lowell asked, growing angry at what the poor young woman must've gone through.

"Yep."

"Why're Mad Buffalo and Whirling Storm lookin' so skittish? Certainly, they can't be bothered by a few bones?"

"Ain't no Injins I know of feel comfortable around the dead. It's just their way." He rose and spoke in Cheyenne with his two Indian friends. They nodded, mounted their ponies and rode off, Mad Buffalo heading the way they were going, Whirling Storm the way they had come. Hudson and the two Cheyennes would not put it past the Comanches to circle back around if they thought they were being followed.

Hudson turned. "Have two of your men dig a grave for that poor chil', Sergeant," he said. "I want it fairly deep, so the wolves and such don't go diggin' it up, though them scavengers seem to have picked her clean already. But I don't wantin' 'em takin' all day at it."

Lowell nodded. After he directed two of the men to begin the digging, he went back to stand next to Hudson. The former mountain man was leaning on his horse, chin resting on arms folded on the saddle. His flickering eyes went from the desolate horizon to the bones and back.

"So," Lowell said quietly, "the Comanches've got, what, almost two days start on us?"

Hudson nodded. "And they're movin' fast."

"You know, Mister Hudson," Lowell said stiffly but flatly, "if we hadn't of taken that night in the Cheyenne village, we might've prevented that poor girl's death."

"I doubt it," Hudson said flatly. The thought had occurred to him, but he was not about to admit it. Still, there was just a little too much truth in Lowell's statement for Hudson's comfort. "Jist 'cause you're feelin' guilty about spendin' some time with a Cheyenne woman, don't you try'n shift that shit over to me."

Lowell couldn't bring himself to argue. It would do no good anyway. The woman was dead. Nothing would bring her back and all the regret in the world wouldn't undo what had occurred.

"How old you think she was?" Lowell asked quietly after a lengthy silence.

Hudson shrugged. "Could've been anywhere from fifteen to fifty, I suppose. Judgin' by the remains, I'd say a heap closer to fifteen than the other."

"Damn," Lowell breathed. "Why would the goddamn Comanches do somethin' like that?"

Hudson glanced at him, eyes red with anger and regret. "You ain't ever known of a white man who'd rape a girl and then kill her?"

"Unfortunately, I do know. I don't know, maybe it's just the surroundings or somethin', but it seems somehow more cruel out here."

"Well, it ain't no worse than havin' it happen in Saint Louis or Taos or Richmond."

"No, I suppose it ain't."

They fell into silence, thinking, until one of the soldiers said, "Sarge, we got the hole dug."

Hudson and Lowell turned. "That good enough, Mister Hudson?" Lowell asked.

"It'll do. And call me Linus."

Lowell nodded. "Gather her bones up, boys, and place 'em in there. And gently, like she was your own sister."

"I wouldn't have no greasy Mexican bitch for a sister," Farmer said with a laugh. Everyone ignored him.

"Any of you boys a Catholic?" Hudson asked.

"I am," a medium-tall, freckle-faced young man said, stepping forward. "Why?"

"I'd be obliged if you were to say some words over the grave. Bein' a Mexican, this girl was a Catholic, and her family'll feel a heap better if she was buried as proper as we can make it."

"I can do that, Mister Hudson." He didn't seem really happy about the prospect, though.

"What's your name, boy?"

"Sean O'Murray."

"Well, Private Sean O'Murray, do your best for her."

"I will, sir."

A moment later, Hudson overheard Farmer say to O'Murray, "I didn't know you were a follower of the goddamn pope."

"You watch your tongue, Gregg Farmer, when it comes to His Holiness."

"Eat shit. Any man who kisses the ass of that devil don't deserve ..." He stopped when O'Murray popped him a shot in the mouth. In the next moment, the two were scrabbling in the dust.

Lowell took a step toward the combatants, but Hudson stopped him. "Let 'em be, Sergeant. We'll step in if it looks to be gettin' too bad."

Lowell nodded. He was generally in favor of the men settling their own disputes. He had thought to break this one up, though, simply because he figured Hudson wanted to get back on the trail as fast as possible. Not that a few minutes would make much difference.

Ten minutes later, Lowell finally stepped in, declared the fight a draw, ordered the two men to get cleaned up and then had them finish up their grisly task. At last, O'Murray said several prayers, in Latin, and the remains of the unfortunate woman were covered.

The men got back into their saddles and rode on. All but Hudson were more somber and more worried. The adventure seemed to have drained out of this mission for the soldiers.

Hudson called a halt around noon, more to give the horses a rest than for the men. While the soldiers tended the animals, Hudson walked back on their trail just a bit and stood there, staring over the dull, mostly flat land.

"Somethin' botherin' you, Linus?" Lowell asked, walking up.

Hudson shrugged. "Just got a feelin' we ain't alone out here."

Lowell made no fun of the statement. He had often felt such premonitions himself. "Comanches?" he asked.

Hudson shrugged again. "Hell if I know." He sighed, wishing he knew what had set his internal alarm off. "Well, I suppose we'll find out after a while."

Linus looked at his companion, and his eyes widened. "You're worried about Whirling Storm, aren't you, Linus?"

Hudson nodded. "He's a good friend. He's been so for a heap of time. I'd be plumb put out was he to go under at the hands of the Comanches because of me."

CHAPTER 7

"Someone's following us," Whirling Storm said when he rode into the little camp.

"I suspected," Hudson said. "Comanches?"

Whirling Storm shrugged as he dismounted. "Not sure. If so, he's alone, which seems strange for a Comanche out here."

"Only one?" Hudson asked, surprised.

Whirling Storm nodded. "As best as I can tell."

"Well, didn't you go check out who it was and what he wanted?"

"Not yet," Whirling Storm said matter of factly. "We're not afraid of a Comanche out there by himself. I'll go see who it is after I've taken care of my pony."

"Didn't you even get close enough to see who he was?" It would never occur to Hudson to leave a job such as this half done, which is how he saw it. He would've found out who the follower was, taken care of him, and then reported back to the others.

Whirling Storm shook his head. "He's a few miles behind, and movin' slow. I don't think he's about to cause trouble. I also think he knows I know he's there. He's staying back just far enough to taunt us, but not close enough that I can get a good look at him."

"Tricky old bastard, isn't he?" Hudson said with a nod. "Go see to your horse and get yourself some water and food."

Lowell had listened to the exchange but had not understood a word of it since the two men had been conversing in Cheyenne. When Whirling Storm left, Lowell asked, "What was that all about, Linus?"

Hudson explained it.

"Are you worried?"

"Nope. If it's only one man, even if he is a Comanche or a Kiowa, he won't cause us any trouble. If he's scoutin' for a larger group, they'll have to show themselves sooner or later. Then we can decide jist what to do about them. It might be he's just keepin' an eye on us to see what we're doin' out here. Whirlin' Storm'll check him out after a spell."

Lowell nodded and left to see about his men.

Soon after, Whirling Storm rode out again, moving slowly to check their back trail—and whoever was following them.

Hudson got the soldiers on the trail again, heading southward yet some more. The land was unerringly dull. The men plodded along, their horses kicking up a small puff of dust with each step. The wind blew unceasingly but it did nothing to alleviate the heat, the boredom, or the dust.

"Where're you plannin' to stay the night, Linus?" Lowell asked sometime during the long, dreary afternoon.

"Probably along Two Butte Creek," Hudson said, figuring Lowell would have no idea what he was talking about.

"Then there'll be water?" Lowell asked hopefully.

"If the gods're smilin' on us and our medicine's strong, we might find a mouthful or two," Hudson responded dryly.

"I thought you said we'd be stayin' along a creek," Lowell remarked, surprised.

"Most of what're called creeks out in these parts're creeks in name only at this time of year, Sergeant. Spring you might find 'em runnin' pretty well, but after the heat and sun've had a summer to work on 'em, they're as likely parched as not."

"Are we all right for water?"

"Reckon so. We don't find any tonight, though, we might have to ration what we got left. There's other creeks we'll be passin' and we should be able to find water in at least one of 'em, even if it means doin' some diggin'."

Lowell nodded, partly assuaged. He thought he could feel the thickness of thirst already clogging his throat, even though he knew it was not really so.

Several hours later, they pulled into a brushy spot along a dry wash. Mad Buffalo was there and had tended his horse. He had gathered some brush and dried buffalo dung to use for fuel and he was skinning two coyotes.

"What're you fixin' to do with them coyotes, Mad Buffalo?" Lowell asked. It was the first time he had really addressed the Cheyenne directly since they had left the village.

"Cook 'em," Mad Buffalo said with a grin. "Eat em.

"Eat 'em?" Lowell asked, face blanching a little.

"Damn good eatin'," Mad Buffalo said.

Lowell looked at Hudson. "He's kiddin', ain't he?"

"Nope," Hudson said with a straight face. "The Cheyennes like fresh dog. A coyote ain't nothin' but a wild dog. Now, me, I prefer pup to some stringy goddamn coyote, but Mad Buffler, that son of a bitch, he'll eat anything." He laughed at the bemused look on his friend's face.

"You ain't gonna get me to eat none of it," Lowell said with finality.

Hudson laughed again. "You git hungry enough, boy, you'll eat coyote shit without flavorin'," he remarked.

They set about making their simple camp and tending the horses. Soon after, Whirling Storm rode in—with Stolen Back Woman in tow.

"Where the hell'd she come from?" Hudson asked.

"She was the one followin' us all along."

"That was a damn fool thing to do, woman," Hudson said, looking up at his wife. She still sat on her pony, and she looked completely unconcerned that Hudson might be angry. "And goddamn dangerous, too."

"Not too dangerous," Whirling Storm threw in. "She was ridin' close enough that we could help her if it became necessary. But not so close that she'd be found too soon."

Hudson nodded. Stolen Back Woman dismounted and Whirling Storm moved off, taking his pony and the woman's with him.

Hudson looked at Stolen Back Woman. "Well, what the hell're you doing here?" he demanded of the woman in a combination of English and Cheyenne.

"I missed you," Stolen Back Woman said, unabashed. She looked almost amused.

"And I missed you," Hudson responded in Cheyenne. "But we're facing some serious trouble here, woman, with what we have to do."

"I've seen trouble before," Stolen Back Woman said flatly. "And I don't like sitting back in the village waiting for you every time you get the idea to go on some crazy adventure like this. It's hard for me, never knowing if I'll ever see you again, never knowing if our son will have a father again. I decided it's time we were together more."

"Oh, you did, did you?" Hudson said, fighting back a chuckle. Hudson could think of no other response to make, really. When she nodded, he tacked on, "Maybe it's time I lodgepoled you."

Stolen Back Woman shrugged, but a smile tickled the corners of her mouth. "Do what you want," she said quietly.

Hudson stared at his woman for some moments. He had never thought of things from her viewpoint before. He felt about the same as she did, but he felt that he was bound—or should be bound—by convention to leave her at the village whenever he went on one of his trips. Such things were no place for a woman. Or were they? He had brought Speckled Pony with him to the mountains years ago when the beaver trade still flourished. There had been no end of danger then, facing Indians of various nations, Mexican soldiers, American scoundrels, wild animals, and more. There was no reason he could see for not bringing Stolen Back Woman along on this trip, other than tradition, and he never had been much of one for tradition.

Hudson shrugged and then nodded. He was happy to have Stolen Back Woman along and he couldn't do anything about it now anyway. "Go on, woman, and start making us something to eat," he said quietly in Cheyenne. "It'll be robe time soon."

"Is there trouble with the Cheyennes, Linus?" Lowell asked when Stolen Back Woman had strolled off. He had been standing silently off to the side watching, knowing he would not be able to understand them, and not wanting to intrude.

"Nope."

"Then what's your wife doin' here?"

"She misses me," Hudson said almost shyly. He was proud of the fact that she did, but he was uncomfortable voicing it.

"And?" Lowell asked warily.

"And so she'll be comin' along from here on," Hudson said flatly.

"I find that rather troublesome, Linus," Lowell said haltingly. He liked Hudson and enjoyed being around the crusty frontiersman, which meant it was difficult for him to give Hudson a hard time about anything.

"So?"

"Well, I don't think this is a woman's place," Lowell said stiffly. "A woman shouldn't have to be subjected to the rigors of trail life and the dangers of our mission."

Hudson almost grinned. "Hell, Sergeant, Stolen Back Woman lives out here. This is her land."

"You know what I mean, Linus."

"I suppose I do, boy," Hudson agreed. "Not that it makes any difference."

"Look, Linus," Lowell said with a sigh, "I've got no real authority to tell you to do anything, but I have to protest this. It just ain't right somehow."

"Right or wrong, Sergeant, she's here and she ain't goin' back now."

"Why?" Lowell asked, surprised.

"We can't afford the time to take her back and we can't afford to send anyone back with her," Hudson said simply.

"Two compelling points," Lowell admitted. He grinned ruefully.

"And I ain't sendin' her back alone," Hudson said with finality.

Lowell nodded, thinking he knew how Hudson felt. "Explainin' this to the men ought to be interestin'."

"Ain't no reason to explain anything," Hudson said a little harshly. "No matter how much grumblin' those goddamn soldier boys of yours do. It's simply the way things are. That's all." He paused. "And if any of 'em becomes a big enough pain in the ass about it, tell him, havin' her along might help us out some."

"How so?" Lowell asked, surprised.

"Most Injins see a woman with a group, they'll figure it ain't a war party. They'll figure we're here for peaceable things." He grinned and winked. "Of course, once the Comanches see them blue coats of yours, they might not be so friendly, woman with us or not."

Lowell nodded, still uncertain about all this. "I still worry that there'll be trouble," he said lamely.

"There ain't gonna be no trouble, Sergeant," Hudson said flatly. "Somebody tries messin' with her, he'll be one sorry son of a bitch. And that'll be before I git my hands on him."

Lowell glanced over at the shapely, pretty young woman and decided Hudson was right. Stolen Back Woman could take care of herself pretty well, he figured, and if she couldn't, then Hudson could. He nodded and even managed another lopsided smile. "I will say, Linus, that she's a sight prettier to look on than any of the rest of us. That brightens things up right there."

The soldiers couldn't complain too much about having Stolen Back Woman along, especially since she almost immediately began cooking for the group. The men quickly found that anything she made— including roast coyote, which even Lowell had forced himself to try—was better than anything they could concoct.

She was also a calming, pleasant presence around their nightly camps and most of the small contingent of soldiers became used to having three Indians, one of them a woman, around.

"Are we makin' any progress, Linus?" Lowell asked on their fourth night out. He was tired and sunburned and his crotch was chafed, all of which put him in a foul mood. Though they had found water when needed, he still seemed to feel dry most of the time, and that added to his irritableness. He knew the same concerns were plaguing his men as well.

"As far as I know, we haven't seen any sign of the missing soldiers, the women, or of any Comanches at all."

"That's the way of things sometimes, Sergeant," Hudson said easily. He knew time was a problem, but he, Mad Buffalo, and Whirling Storm were doing all they could. Short of having the Comanches ride up and tell them where the captives were, all Hudson and the others could do was to continue their hunt. "We can look for days or weeks and not find anything, and then we might walk right in on a camp of Comanches who're holdin' your friends."

"That doesn't sound very reliable."

"It's the best can be done, Sergeant. Take a look around you, boy. What do you see?"

"Nothin'." He hadn't seen anything—except his traveling companions and an occasional hawk—since they had crossed the river. Just miles and miles of windswept, baking, brittle emptiness.

"That's a fact. This ain't like back in the settlements, where there are people all over. Back there, you can talk to 'em and maybe get some information. Out here, though, all you can do is look for signs in the dirt and maybe in the wind and the sky."

"Not a whole lot to go on, is it?"

"Nope," Hudson said bluntly. "We can turn back, if you're of a mind to, boy. Wouldn't bother me none.

I can think of better places to spend my time than out in this hellacious goddamn place. We can be back in a couple, three days. Once we got there, we could tell your Colonel Kearny that we couldn't find those missin' boys and that we figure they were put under straight off by those damned Comanches. Or, if you think it'll sit better with those pompous shit sticks back there, we can tell 'em we found the remains of them boys and buried 'em right there."

Lowell surveyed the night's small camp, with the flickering fire of buffalo chips, the soldiers talking quietly to each other, the horses clumped together, shuffling unconcerned, the three Cheyennes chatting and laughing around their own little fire. Then he shook his head. "I reckon it's too early for that yet. We don't find any sign of them in another week, though, and I'll consider doin' either one of those things you just spoke of."

"We can cover a far piece of country in a week was we of a mind to, Sergeant."

"Then let's plan to do so—unless we find them soon."

"Your boys're gonna git saddle sore, Sergeant," Hudson said with a grin.

"They'll survive," Lowell responded grimly.

"Will you?" Hudson asked bluntly.

Lowell raised his eyebrows in Hudson's direction. He didn't think that deserved the dignity of an answer. He did wonder, though, if he would be up to what was going to be asked of him.

CHAPTER 8

Lowell dismounted and rubbed the seat of his pants. After four solid eighteen-hour days in the saddle, he was not even sure he had an ass left. He felt as if he had been riding on nothing but his tailbone for at least a day. He looked around and decided that at least they had a halfway decent place to spend the night this time.

Their campsite was along the Canadian River deep in the Llano Estacado. Cottonwoods and a few willows lined the bank here, offering shade from the brutal assault of the sun. There was green grass around, so the animals had so good forage for a change, and the water was cool and refreshing.

Hudson watched Lowell for a few moments. His respect for the sergeant had grown considerably in the more than a week they had been on the trail. He had found Lowell to be a good man. He took all that was dished out and never complained, which was a lot more than could be said of some of the other soldiers, Farmer and McKagan in particular.

The two had grumbled considerably, especially after Hudson began pushing the men hard. It annoyed Hudson no end.

Hudson figured it was inevitable that he and Farmer would have a serious set-to, but he hoped to avoid it until at least they got the missing soldiers and women back—or buried them; but he didn't know if that would be possible. Farmer grated on his nerves almost constantly.

He shrugged the gloomy feeling off and finished tending his horse. He could sympathize with Lowell some. His own rear end was sore and he was a lot more used to long hours in the saddle than Lowell was.

Mad Buffalo had downed a buffalo calf that afternoon and so they had good eating awaiting them as soon as their chores were done. Because of that, everyone hurried to finish, and then sat and eagerly began bolting down hunks of calf meat.

The small camp had two fires, one at which Hudson, Lowell, and the three Cheyennes sat, and a second which had the six privates. Each had meat roasting and a large coffeepot sitting on stones over the real wood fire for a change.

Finally, even the seemingly insatiable Hudson, Whirling Storm and Mad Buffalo were done eating. The three lit up pipes and puffed quietly. Lowell pulled out the next to last of his cigars and fired it up. "Seems like the right time for it," he said with a touch of regret in his voice.

They were silent for a while, until Lowell finally asked, "Your wife has an odd—well, odd for me— name, Linus. How'd she come by it? If you don't mind my askin'."

"You got to get out of this habit of apologizin' for askin' things, boy," Hudson said, a little annoyed at it. He found it the most irritating of Lowell's little idiosyncrasies. Actually, he figured it was just his general crankiness at Farmer, McKagan, the futility of their mission, and other such irritants that made him take some umbrage at Lowell's small foible.

Lowell shrugged. "I'd heard that men like you don't take kindly to personal questions. Especially from strangers."

"Reckon that's all true," Hudson acknowledged. "But we ain't strangers no more. We've ridden together some days and you ought to know by now I don't object to such." He grinned a little. "And if I do, you'll know about it straight off."

"All right," Lowell said with a small, slow smile, "how'd your wife get her name?"

"Well now, Injins often change their names. More often the warriors than the women, of course. Somethin' out of the ordinary happens to 'em, they'll change their name. Maybe they'll have a special vision or somethin', or a battle where they've done somethin' particularly heroic, which," he added with a large grin, "is jist about every goddamn battle they've ever been in."

Hudson saw that the other soldiers at the other fire were listening while trying to pretend they weren't. The frontiersman considered embellishing the story some for the troops, but then he decided the tale didn't need it. "It was maybe six years ago, just as the beaver trade was gaspin' its last breaths."

***

Hudson had accompanied a group of the Cheyenne men on a buffalo hunt, leaving his two children at the village. His first wife, Speckled Pony, had died the year before and Hudson was in the market for a new wife. In the meantime, his children were living with an aunt and uncle in the village.

When the men returned from the successful hunt, they found that the village had been raided by Pawnees. Several men had been killed and a number of women and children had been taken captive.

A war party under the leadership of Red Hand was hastily organized. Mad Buffalo and Whirling Storm immediately announced they were going along. The latter had been on his first war party the previous summer, the former had gone just this year for the first time. Both were eager for more action, for the chance to earn honors and glory, and maybe even a little plunder, making their quest for wives that much easier.

Having nothing else he had to be doing, Hudson announced that he, too, would go along for the ride. It never hurt when one could remove a few hated Pawnees from the bosom of Mother Earth, he always thought.

They had ridden out of the village within an hour of having ridden in from the hunt and seen the damage. The Pawnees had only about four hours' head start on them, and, hampered by their captives, were moving rather slowly, though steadily. And, while Red Hand's painted, grim-faced Cheyennes moved fast, the Pawnees showed no signs of stopping anytime soon.

The Cheyenne war party had ridden throughout the night and caught up to the Pawnees about an hour after dawn the next day. Two Cheyenne scouts galloped back to the main body to say they had spotted the Pawnees out across the openness of the prairie less than half a mile ahead.

The Cheyennes moved on another quarter of a mile and then divided into two groups. One group headed southeast, the other northeast. Both rode hard, whipping their ponies. Two miles on, they stopped, forming a loose arc directly in the path of the Pawnees. They dismounted and several boys gathered up the horses, which they herded behind another low, grassy ridge a hundred yards or so behind where one section of the living arc curled around to the north and west. There the boys would hold the ponies in readiness. The dismounted warriors lay in the tall, waving grass under the brutal sun, watching, waiting.

As the Pawnees hove into view, the Cheyennes had suddenly jumped up, firing arrows, and screeching war cries. Hudson was right among them, firing his single-shot pistol, then grabbing his tomahawk and wading into the thick of the battle.

A Pawnee rode his pony into Hudson, knocking him down and heavily bruising his chest and shoulder. Hudson rolled out of the way of the horse's hooves and then lurched upright. He headed toward the still-mounted warrior but then Whirling Storm suddenly materialized on the horse, just behind the warrior. The young Cheyenne grabbed the Pawnee's greasy roached hair and began sliding his knife across his forehead.

The Pawnee jerked his head back, hitting Whirling Storm's face hard. Then he rammed an elbow into Whirling Storm's ribs. The Cheyenne began sliding off the horse. Another elbow from the Pawnee gave him the final impetus to knock him to the ground.

Whirling Storm would not release his grip on the Pawnee's hair, though, and he pulled the enemy down with him. The ground broke Whirling Storm's grasp and the young Cheyenne grunted from the impact. As the two Indians landed, Hudson stepped forward and stomped on the Pawnee's throat. Then he split the Indian's skull.

Hudson winked at Whirling Storm. "You counted first coup on him, boy, you raise his hair." Then he had turned and moved off into the swirling cloud of dust, noise, and confusion.

Hudson had waded through the ranks of fighting Cheyennes and Pawnees, fighting when he had to, pulling women and children with him when he could. He would send the women on their way right off, but he kept the children with him. The women could, for the most part, fend for themselves; the children could not, and none would protect the young ones better than the gentle but still-fearsome Fierce Bear.

Before long, Hudson had a small herd of young rescued captives along with him and he began making his way out of the melee to get his charges to safety. Finally, he broke through the edge of the whirling clouds of confusion and he could breathe without choking on the dust.

"Come on, children," Hudson said in Cheyenne, urging them on, "over the ridge. You'll be safe there."

Other rescued captives were on the far side of the ridge, under the watchful eyes of some of the Cheyenne warriors. Hudson let the children join their mothers and friends. He spotted Mad Buffalo just arriving and walked over to him.

"The Pawnees are on the run," Mad Buffalo crowed, face streaked with paint and sweat.

"The fightin's over?" Hudson asked, running a greasy sleeve across his forehead.

"Almost. The Pawnees are dogs. They couldn't stand against us for long. Now they're running, except the ones who're trapped and who're fighting desperately to get free. They won't, though."

Hudson nodded. "You going back to raise more hair?" he asked.

"Of course," Mad Buffalo said. There had never been any question of that, and he was surprised that Hudson had even asked.

"May your medicine remain strong, little brother," Hudson said, sending Mad Buffalo on his way. Hudson turned and found his canteen. Then he sat in a relatively quiet spot and sipped water, letting the Cheyennes proceed with their bloody business. He was not, by nature, a bloodthirsty man and while he had raised his share of hair and more, he saw no reason to join in the butchering of the Pawnees. That might be the Cheyennes' way, but it wasn't his. His friends among the People knew that and understood it.

It was only a half hour or so before all the Cheyennes were back, clutching bloody trophies in their hands, shouting in their exultation. The Pawnees had been wiped out to a man, they figured, and all the captives had been rescued. This without a single Cheyenne casualty. There was good cause to rejoice.

Finally, they began their procession home. Some of the children were doubled and even tripled on ponies, so they moved slowly. There was no need to rush now.

They were almost back to the village when consternation broke out near the front of the line. It worked its way rapidly toward the back. Hudson rode near the rear, off to the side a little, feeling a little out of place among the Cheyennes, as he had since Speckled Pony had died.

"What's wrong?" Hudson asked Whirling Storm, who trotted up and stopped his pony next to Hudson.

"At least three captives were not found," Whirling Storm replied in Cheyenne. Like his companions, he was highly agitated. "Two children and a woman— Eating the Moon. We didn't realize until now."

"Think they were killed?"

Whirling Storm shook his head. "We saw no sign of it."

"A couple of Pawnee bucks got away with them during the fighting," Hudson said more than asked.

"That's what I think."

"You sending someone after them?"

"That's what the argument's about," Whirling Storm said with a reluctant grin. "Red Hand wants to push on to the village and make sure everyone is safe first. Others want to go after them."

Hudson nodded. He had nothing better to do these days, so he said, "You go tell Red Hand that me and you'll go chase them down. I wouldn't mind the company of a couple others if they wanted to come along, but not too many."

Whirling Storm's face brightened, and he nodded. He galloped off but returned soon with Mad Buffalo. "This is all who'll come," Whirling Storm said.

"Suits me," Hudson said in English. "Let's move."

They followed their trail back again, heading eastward. They made a cold camp that night and were up and moving again before dawn. Late in the morning, they finally came to the spot where the battle with the Pawnees had taken place. They split up and began scouring the ground around the fringes of the battlefield, looking for sign.

Mad Buffalo was the one who found it and he had done so in moments. The other two joined him and the three pressed on as fast as they could manage. Several hours later, they came on a Pawnee body, partly ravaged by scavengers.

Whirling Storm knelt and surveyed the ground around it, then looked up at his two companions. "Only the Pawnee's here," he said in Cheyenne.

"Well, what happened, goddammit?" Hudson asked with a snort.

"Someone killed this dog of a Pawnee and took the woman and the children away."

"Who?"

Whirling Storm rose and shrugged. "White men.

At least three."

"Well, let's get to followin' 'em," Hudson said. "They can't be too far ahead."

Two hours later, they first heard, then saw, a small wagon, the ungreased wheels of which created an unholy racket. As they closed in, the three could see that there were three men mounted and another walking along by the cart. They were still too far to see if the Cheyenne woman and two children were there.

They rode into a gully that paralleled the cart and pushed on hard. Then Hudson said, "You two wait here and keep an eye on things."

"We want to go, too."

"I reckon it'll be better for this ol' chil' to go down there by himself. There's no tellin' what those shit sticks'll do if they see a couple Injins."

Hudson moseyed up over the ridge and headed toward the squawking cart and the four men. One of those finally spotted him and the little procession ground to a halt. Everyone exchanged pleasantries when Hudson stopped a few feet from the other men. Eating the Moon and the two children were sitting on the top of the rickety pile of goods in the cart.

"That there's my woman and children," Hudson said, pointing with the rifle in his right hand.

"That so?" one of the men responded. He was a short, heavyset man with stubbled, flaccid features.

"Yep. She was took from me by some Pawnees. I been followin' 'em for a couple of days now. I saw one of them Pawnees killed not far from here. I figure you boys done that and rescued my woman and young'ns. And for that I'm mighty obliged. Now, I'd like to take my family, though, and head on back west."

"That so?" the same man said.

"Yep."

"That woman's mine," the man said. "The brats, too." He spit off the side of his horse. "Less'n you think you can take 'em from me." It was a challenge.

"Looks like you got me outnumbered, friend," Hudson said easily. "Ain't no Injin woman and kids worth gettin' put under for. Sorry to have taken up your time." Hudson turned his horse and began walking it away. Somehow he knew that Mad Buffalo and Whirling Storm were nearby. He suddenly stopped and whirled, bringing up his rifle. He fired, killing the man who had spoken.

The two other mounted men went down seconds afterward, struck by arrows. The man on foot dropped his whip and fled, running across the prairie.

Mad Buffalo and Whirling Storm stood in the grass and waved to Hudson. Then they went to get their horses.

Hudson went to the cart and helped the woman and children down. "You all right?" he asked.

Eating the Moon nodded.

When they got back to the village, Hudson and Eating the Moon—who happily changed her name to Stolen Back Woman—were married.

CHAPTER 9

They crossed the Canadian River the next day and cut cross country away from it, heading south and a little east. Only an occasional deep, narrow canyon broke the utter monotony of the landscape. There was nothing to relieve the travelers of the heat and sandy wind.

By noon, when they stopped to give the horses a short rest, they had come to a mostly dried up stream. There they found the remains of a Comanche camp. "It's a day and a half old," Mad Buffalo announced after scouting it a little. "Maybe a bit more."

"Was it the ones we're after?" Hudson asked.

Mad Buffalo nodded without hesitation.

"How can you tell?" Lowell asked skeptically.

Mad Buffalo waved the sergeant over. When Lowell had knelt next to him, Mad Buffalo pointed. "Boot tracks," he said in English. "Just like yours."

Lowell nodded and looked up at Hudson. "These boys know their business, don't they?"

"Yep." Hudson dismounted. "We'll track 'em down

soon's we've let the horses have a little rest."

They unsaddled the horses and rubbed them down before letting them drink what little water they could find in the creek bed. Not knowing when they might get another chance to eat, the humans gnawed down pieces of beef and buffalo jerky. Stagnant water from pools in the creek bed washed the leathery, stringy meat down.

Finally, they resaddled their horses and pushed on, following San Juan Creek. Mad Buffalo and Whirling Storm rode only a quarter-mile or so ahead of the main group this time, since they soon began seeing unmistakable signs of a larger Comanche camp—discarded food, refuse, cropped-down grass, fire rings, places where meat racks had stood, and more.

Late in the afternoon, the two Cheyenne warriors rode back and indicated that the group should camp where it was.

"You spot a Comanche camp?" Hudson asked.

Mad Buffalo nodded. "Less than a mile up the creek, where it joins the Canadian," he said.

"The soldiers there?" Lowell asked nervously. His men were watching and listening intently.

Mad Buffalo shrugged. "We didn't get close enough to tell."

"Why not?" Lowell asked. He wasn't so much angry as he was plain mystified.

"Bad medicine."

"Bad medicine?" Farmer snorted. "What the fuck does that mean?"

"It means," Hudson said coldly, "that things

weren't right for them going into that village."

"What kind of things weren't right, Linus?" Lowell asked.

"Could be anything," Hudson said. "Injins—all Injins—are mighty superstitious. Things don't seem right to 'em, they back off right away. Doesn't matter how insignificant that something might be. To them, their medicine's gone bad and they'll go at it again another time."

Lowell nodded. He didn't like it, but he was willing to accept it—for now. "When will their medicine be good for seeing if the soldiers are in that Comanche camp?" he asked politely.

"I'll go to the village and ask about the blue coats tomorrow," Whirling Storm said.

Lowell nodded again. "I must confess I don't understand any of this but if you give me your word, Whirling Storm, I'll leave it at that."

"Sounds like a chickenshit excuse to me," Farmer offered snidely.

Mad Buffalo turned a stone-cold face toward Farmer and his fingers edged toward his war club. Suddenly he laughed, a deep, rich, but cold sound. "You're a funny sumbitch for a blue coat," he said, using more of an accent than he really needed. "That's a good goddamn joke." Then his face froze. "But don't make a joke like it again."

The making of the camp had come to a standstill, as everyone looked from the Cheyenne to the soldier.

"Or what?" Farmer asked cockily.

"Or I'll kill you, blue coat sumbitch," Mad Buffalo said flatly. He glared at Farmer another moment before turning back to care for his horse.

"Shit," Farmer said loudly. He was relieved but didn't want anyone else to know it. "Goddamn uppity redskin."

"That'll be enough out of you, Private Farmer," Lowell snapped. The sergeant knew Farmer well enough to know he was all bluster. "Or I'll turn Mad Buffalo loose on you."

"You wouldn't dare," Farmer hissed, eyes wide with hate and fear.

"No tellin' what I might do out here away from the bounds of civilization, Private," Lowell said with a shrug.

"Besides," Hudson added, "Sergeant Lowell don't have no control over Mad Buffler. My amigo there goes for you, the sergeant ain't gonna stop him." He seemed almost jovial.

"Your time's gonna come, you dumb bastard," Farmer said, glaring at Hudson.

"Any time you think you got the balls to come against me, shit stick, have at it. Till then, keep your big mouth shut."

"Kiss my ass, Hudson," Farmer snorted. He was sure he had the upper hand here, simply because he was among fellow soldiers.

Suddenly Mad Buffalo roared up on Farmer, screeching like a maniac. He stopped with his war club an inch from Farmer's cowering head. Then Mad Buffalo grinned and backed off. "You make another good joke," he said, pointing to the spreading wet spot on the front of Farmer's trousers. "Piss in your pants to scare off the enemy with the stink. Funny." He walked away, shaking his head and laughing.

Farmer, who had fallen, rose. His face was a hideous mask of rage and humiliation. Seeing the lack of sympathy on the other soldiers' faces, as well as the smile Hudson was sporting, did nothing to lessen his fury.

"Now that you've made a complete ass of yourself, Private," Lowell said, trying not to sound too condescending, "you have work to do. Get to it."

Farmer was so enraged that he could say nothing; he only sputtered. Then he moved off, walking stiffly.

"There's gonna be trouble over this, Linus," Lowell said as the rest of the men began going about their duties.

Hudson shrugged. "Farmer's got a right to be an asshole jist like any other man," he opined. "Of course, another man's got every right to take exception to it. It's up to them to sort out the particulars." He paused and then grinned as if a thought had suddenly pleased him. "I'll tell you what, though, Sergeant, that shit stick Farmer comes against me or Mad Buffler, he's gonna be dick deep in 'gator-infested waters."

Lowell grinned back a little. "Truth to tell, Linus, it wouldn't mean a damn thing to me to leave his festerin' carcass bleachin' out here in the sun somewhere."

"I'll keep that in mind."

"Don't read more into it than's there, Linus. I ain't lookin' for you or anyone else to kill Farmer. It just wouldn't bother me none if it happened along the way."

Hudson looked Lowell square in the eyes. "I can about guarantee you, Sergeant, that Mister Farmer ain't gonna make it back to Bent's Fort alive. Not if he keeps up his grumblin' and his troublemakin'."

Lowell nodded. He was a little sad, knowing it was true. He had no liking for Private Gregg Farmer but he hated to see any man die because of his own stupidity. And he was quite certain that that was exactly what was going to happen to Farmer.

Their camp did not take long to make since they would have no fires. Hudson and the two Cheyennes did not want to give their position away to the Comanches. They felt it better to know where the Comanche camp was without the Comanches knowing where they were. At least for now.

Since they had had a number of very long days in the saddle, Hudson encouraged them all to turn in early. Whirling Storm was named to take the first watch over the horses, Mad Buffalo the second, and Hudson the hours nearest the dawn.

Hudson always slept like a cat. It was an ability he had seen in many of the men who had made their living—and, more importantly, survived at it— by taking beaver in the icy streams of the Rocky Mountains back in the old days. It had served him well then, and it served him well now, as he was awake at the slightest sound. He knew instinctively that it was not yet quite time for him to take over the watching of the horses, so it had to be something else.

It became evident in moments that it was someone creeping through the camp. It did not fit in with the normal sounds of a night camp—horses shuffling, snores, the rustling of blanket or robe against dry grass. It was someone moving around and trying with little success to be stealthy about it.

Hudson became aware that Stolen Back Woman had woke, too, and was lying quietly while he figured out what was wrong. He rolled a little and whispered into her ear a moment. Then he kissed her lightly, scooped up his Colt Patersons and rose, silent as the night itself.

He moved through the camp, instinctively heading toward the sound. In moments, he spotted a figure creeping low to the ground. The figure seemed to be heading toward where Mad Buffalo would spread his robes when he came off of watching the horses.

Hudson shifted and shoved the pistols away. He moved more swiftly now, aiming to head off the secretive figure that was moving along on all fours.

Private Gregg Farmer never knew Hudson was there until the former mountain man suddenly rose up beside him and kicked him in the side. Farmer hit on his other side, emitting a soft oof and rolled onto his back.

Hudson swiftly knelt, knee in Farmer's stomach, one hand over the soldier's mouth. The other hand held the tip of a big bowie knife to the underside of Farmer's jaw.

"You got no business crawlin' 'round here in the middle of the night, boy," Hudson whispered. "And if you want to live to see the dawn shine, you'll slither your ass back to your bedroll and keep it there till Sergeant Lowell wakes it in the mornin'. That sound reasonable to you, boy?"

Farmer was furious again but he managed to control himself long enough to nod as much as possible with the hard hand on his face.

"I know you was made a fool of today, boy," Hudson said easily. "And that ain't a thing any man takes lightly to. I can understand that, boy. But skulkin' 'round in the middle of the night tryin' to get revenge by stabbin' the object of your hate ain't much of a manly thing neither. I suggest that if you want to git your vengeance against Mad Buffler, that you wait till we're done with this here adventure and then go agin' him man to man. Unless you're too chickenshit for such doin's. In which case, jist let things rest."

Farmer muttered something against Hudson's hand, and the former mountain man removed it. "I ain't afraid of that goddamn redskin," Farmer hissed.

"Then he'll be glad to oblige you face to face— once these here doin's are over. Unless you want to argue some more." Hudson moved the knife fractionally, drawing attention to it.

"I'll wait," Farmer said, trying to battle back the blinding rage that ate at his insides.

Hudson suddenly vanished or so it seemed to Farmer. Hudson was on his chest one minute and then he was alone. He shuddered, thinking the scout unnerving, almost otherworldly. Then he rose and walked off a little, urinated, and returned to his bedroll. It took him some time to get back to sleep though.

In the morning, Whirling Storm and Mad Buffalo

prepared themselves carefully. They wore their finest clothes and painted their faces and ponies. Then, with Stolen Back Woman, they rode out, heading up the brushy creek bank toward the Comanche village.

The others waited. It seemed interminable in the heat with the dry wind rustling the dried brush and grasses. There was little to do and the men found themselves glancing toward where the travelers had gone every few minutes.

A few hours later, the three Cheyennes finally returned. Hudson could see the story on their unhappy faces.

"Those blue coats aren't there?" Hudson asked in Cheyenne.

Whirling Storm shrugged. "It doesn't matter even if they are," he answered in his own language. "The Comanches wouldn't give them to us anyway. We must make ready to fight."

"What's he sayin'?" Lowell asked urgently. He knew something was wrong, but he had no idea what.

Hudson explained it.

"Fight?" Lowell burst out. "I thought you said the Cheyennes and the Comanches were allies, Linus."

"They are. Generally."

"Then what the hell's wrong?" Lowell was befuddled.

"They call us enemies 'cause Mad Buffalo and I brought you other blue coats here," Whirling Storm said flatly.

"But that's preposterous! I mean, they ..."

"It don't make no goddamn difference now, boy,"

Hudson said. "Here they come." He pointed.

Twenty or so Comanche warriors were racing on horseback toward them.

Suddenly Lowell was an army sergeant again. He had never really fought Indians before but he knew what had to be done. He whirled. "Linus, can Stolen Back Woman watch the horses with one of my men?"

"Yep." Hudson saw the sense of it right off. That way they'd only have to spare one fighting man instead of two.

"Private Hogg," Lowell commanded, "get the horses down in that little hollow over there and watch 'em with the Injin woman. The rest of you spread out, take cover. Fire only on my orders or the orders of Mister Hudson."

Mad Buffalo and Whirling Storm had already disappeared into the brush and Hudson slid into position on a large, circular, semi-flat rock, rifle ready. The rock was canted upward a little away from the creek bank, so he got a clearer view of the battlefield.

"Mind if I join you?" Lowell asked as he slithered up the rock alongside Hudson.

"Nope." Hudson glanced over at Lowell and grinned. "Think you're ready for a little Injin fightin'?" he asked.

"Nope," Lowell answered seriously.

CHAPTER 10

A withering fire from the soldiers and Cheyennes split the Comanches on the first run, dropping at least three of the attacking warriors.

"That's showin' those redskin bastards," one of the soldiers shouted as the Comanches trotted off, carrying their dead and wounded.

"They'll be back," Hudson warned as he calmly reloaded his heavy rifle.

"Report!" Lowell shouted.

Six soldiers responded, each with a simple, "All right."

"Whirlin' Storm?" Hudson called. "How're you and Mad Buffler?"

"Bueno," Mad Buffalo shouted back.

"Stolen Back Woman?"

"Fine," the woman called out. "The horses, too."

Hudson cocked his head as several bird calls rippled out. Then he nodded and made some of the same sounds.

"Signals?" Lowell asked quietly.

"Yep. Those Comanches ain't gonna come at us in the open again like that. Whirlin' Storm and Mad Buffler'll be movin' around out in the grass there, tryin' to keep the Comanches from sneakin' up on your soldier boys too easy."

"Could the Comanches do that?"

"Hell, yes. These ain't some asswhipped poor devil Injins like them back east. These here are mean, asskickin' Injins. Ones with a heap of balls and, more important, a heap of brains when it comes to fightin'."

"Sounds like you like them."

"I got no particular likin' for the bastards, really," Hudson commented. "No particular dislikin' for 'em either. But I do respect 'em. Some others learned to do that, there might be less trouble. There ain't no reason to hate those boys out there. Just like there ain't no reason to fear 'em. They're jist tryin' to get on with their lives jist like you and me. Trouble is, we and them got us different goals. That's where the conflict comes in. I... "

Hudson had never taken his eyes off the land in front of him. Suddenly he whistled once like a bird. An answer came back and he suddenly fired.

"What the . . . ?" Lowell started, but then he realized that the response Hudson had gotten must have been the wrong one. Besides, it was too late to worry about that now, as a Comanche popped up right in front of him. Trouble was, it was so surprising that Lowell was not quite prepared to handle it.

Hudson's one hand snaked out and latched on

the back of Lowell's uniform blouse. Then Hudson rolled onto his back and started sliding off the rock, pulling Lowell with him.

A Comanche lance point cracked on the rock where a moment before the sergeant's body had been. Hudson stopped sliding and managed to get half up on one knee. He fired three shots from one Colt Paterson. Three lead balls popped into the Comanche's bare, brownish chest and the Indian fell.

Other gunfire erupted from around the camp and there were some war whoops as well as shouted curses in English. Then silence settled over the soldiers' camp again.

"You all right?" Hudson asked calmly.

"Yessir. Sorry, I just..."

"Check on your men," Hudson ordered. He was not interested in explanations right now. He knew what the sergeant was going through and they didn't have time anyway. He slithered back up to his rock, noting with a little admiration that Lowell was right behind him.

"Report!" Lowell bellowed. He was sweating from the heat and from fear. He felt he had failed himself and, worse, failed Hudson. He was suddenly worried that he might not be the man he had always thought—or hoped—he was.

He got five "all rights" and one "vounded, Sergeant." The latter was from Private Helmut Hochner.

"How bad?" Lowell called, a sinking feeling in his stomach.

"I'll liff veil enough to fight another day," Hochner

said strongly.

"Whirlin' Storm?" Hudson called. He got no answer. He called again, his heart seeming to stop as the seconds ticked by. He relaxed a little when he heard the call of a cardinal. He was a little worried, though, since it was faint and sort of faraway sounding. He finally decided it was because Whirling Storm had gotten within the Comanche ranks.

"Mad Buffler?" Hudson called.

"Fine." Mad Buffalo then chattered out some rapid-fire Cheyenne.

"What's he gonna do?" Lowell asked when Hudson had acknowledged Mad Buffalo.

"You jist stay here and watch." Hudson slid off the rock and soon was lost in the brush. He stopped some yards off and grabbed a tuft of dried grass and sort of tied it in a knot. He pulled out a match, scratched it to life and then lit the knotted grass in his hand. When it was burning well, he jumped up tossed it. Fifty yards away, he saw Mad Buffalo doing the same thing.

Hudson ducked back down as fire started in the dried grass that ran from the lightly sloping creek bank to the prairie that stretched out to forever. Within moments, clouds of smoke were boiling up, and flames were reaching out toward the prairie, pushed by the winds coming from the direction of the soldiers' camp. Hudson hurried back to his rock and knelt there. "Best git ready, Sergeant," he said.

Out of the smoke came Comanches, charging forward on foot, silent, blackened by the fire, ready to overrun the small camp.

Hudson shoved Lowell out of the way as a short, burly Comanche barreled forward. The move allowed the warrior's lance to slice across Hudson's side, though not very deeply.

"Son of a bitch," Hudson breathed as the fire of pain rippled through his flesh. He clamped his arm down on the shaft of the spear, snaring it against his bleeding side and he half spun. At the same time, he ripped out a pistol and clubbed the Comanche on the side of the head with it.

The Comanche sagged a little and Hudson slapped the pistol alongside his head again. As the warrior sank to his knees, groggy, Hudson thumbed back the revolver's hammer and shot him pointblank through the left temple. A moment later Hudson let the lance drop on top of the Indian's body.

Hudson turned just in time to have another Comanche slam into him, knocking him backward and down the little slope. He grunted and whistled as he and the warrior rolled through several thorny bushes and then landed with a light splat in a small mud puddle in the creek bed.

Hudson wrestled the Comanche off him and was about ready to plunge his knife into the Indian's chest when he realized the warrior was already dead, with a gaping wound front and back. Hudson looked down at himself and saw he, too, had another wound—a short puncture in his abdomen. It didn't seem to be too deep, and he couldn't figure out what it was from. He shrugged. It didn't matter, now. He slogged up the hill to his rock but the soldiers and the two Cheyennes had driven the Comanches off.

Hudson stopped next to Lowell, puffing a little from the exertion. The sergeant was standing there with his single-shot pistol in one hand and his short army-issued sword in the other. Hudson suddenly realized where he had gotten his second wound. "Best be careful with that goddamn thing, Sergeant," he said, waving a revolver at the sword.

Lowell nodded blankly, almost as if he hadn't heard. Then he began regaining his senses. He checked on his men. Hochner had been wounded a second time, though he was still not bad off, and Private Sean O'Murray had taken an arrow in the thigh. Hudson seemed none the worse for his two small wounds. Then they spotted Whirling Storm, who came staggering back into the camp.

Mad Buffalo grabbed his friend as he fell and eased him to the ground. Mad Buffalo looked up at Hudson with worry set in his deep brown eyes.

Whirling Storm was covered with blood. He was cut in several places and had at least two arrow wounds. Hudson knelt next to him. "This doesn't look good, my friend," he said in Cheyenne. "Looks like your time to go to the Great Spirit's just about here."

Whirling Storm nodded a little. There was pain in his eyes, but no fear. "Dying doesn't worry me," he said. He looked at Mad Buffalo. "You will take in Smiling Spirit?"

"I'll honor her as much as my first wife," Mad Buffalo said firmly.

Whirling Storm nodded and looked back at Hudson. "Where are the Comanches?"

"Still out there, waitin'."

"Let me rest a little," Whirling Storm said quietly. He seemed resolved to death and appeared to be at peace with it. "Then I'll challenge them."

"You sure?"

"Yes."

Hudson nodded. He called to Stolen Back Woman and instructed her to care for Whirling Storm as best she could. He stood then and walked back up the rise a little to where the land flattened out to stretch to the horizon. He reloaded his rifle and then his pistol, all the while watching the Comanches bunched up out there in the distance.

Lowell tentatively joined him after a few minutes. "Whirling Storm's dyin', ain't he?"

"Yep." Hudson's voice was cold.

"Nothin' can be done for him?"

"Nope."

"What happens next?"

"We wait."

"For what?" Lowell was suddenly worried. His small group was still outnumbered and Hudson had suddenly seemed to have turned against him.

"We wait," Hudson repeated. He leaned his rifle against his stomach and pulled out some tobacco. Chewing, he lifted his rifle again and rested it across his shoulders, hands draped loosely over each end. His face, watching the Comanches, was hard.

After what seemed like a long time, Mad Buffalo helped Whirling Storm up to where Hudson and Lowell still waited. "You ready, boy?" Hudson asked roughly in English.

Whirling Storm nodded and even managed a small, one-sided smile. "It's good for a young man to die on such a day," he said softly, honestly, in his own language. "The sun is warm on my face and my spirit is at peace. I have my two best friends to watch my glory."

"Well, that fills me with no end of good feelings," Hudson said sarcastically in Cheyenne. "Just keep thinking of yourself, you selfish young fool."

Whirling Storm smiled a little again. "You're just jealous it's not your honor to go to the Great Spirit today."

"I can wait my turn." Hudson spit tobacco juice, wishing for all the world that there was something he could do to change this. But there wasn't and he damn well knew it. He was just stalling. "You have what you need, brother?"

Whirling Storm nodded.

"See you in the spirit land one day, my friend," he said. He gently hugged Whirling Storm and then released him.

Whirling Storm went through the ritual with Mad Buffalo and then began walking slowly, steadily toward the Comanches.

"Where's he goin', Linus?" Lowell asked in wonder and worry. "What's goin' on?"

"Watch," Hudson said, voice cracking with emotion.

A weakening Whirling Storm finally stopped. He draped a long, painted strap across one shoulder, then hammered the end of it to the ground with a wooden stake. Tugging on the leather to make sure the stake was firmly settled, he walked to the edge of his line.

"Goddammit, Linus, tell me what this is all about," Lowell said desperately.

"Whirlin' Storm knows he's dyin' and that he ain't got a hope in hell of savin' himself," Hudson said in a voice deepened with grief. "He aims to sell his life as dearly, as bravely, and with as much goddamn glory as possible. He'll stand out there alone, not moving beyond that length of buckskin and challenge the fuckin' Comanches. Then he'll take out as many as he goddamn can before they put him down for good."

"That's crazy." Lowell was stunned almost beyond belief.

"Not to Whirlin' Storm. Or the Comanches. The enemy'll admire Whirlin' Storm's bravery. Maybe they'll even sing about him around the fires for a time. It won't stop them from killin' him, but they'll admire him for it. And it might even inspire a few of them boys to show the same goddamn spirit when their time comes."

"And you won't help him?" Lowell could not believe that.

"No." Hudson's voice sounded as if it came from a grave somewhere.

"But..."

"Shut the fuck up and watch," Hudson ordered roughly.

Comanches were heading toward Whirling Storm already. They were moving warily, admiring the young Cheyenne's bravery, wanting to allow him to sing his death song a bit, to recount his courage before the end came. They could respect that.

Hudson watched with eyes clouded by tears as six Comanches suddenly charged Whirling Storm. The fight was short, fierce, and bloody before Whirling Storm went down for the last time. Still, he took two Comanches to the afterworld with him and wounded three others. The Comanches would not soon forget this courageous, honorable Cheyenne.

CHAPTER 11

Sergeant Alfred Lowell gasped when he saw one of the Comanches kneel and bend over Whirling Storm's body. The Comanche had a knife in his hand. A moment later the Comanche's head exploded in a shower of blood, bone, and brain matter. Lowell looked over at Hudson, mouth agape.

Hudson was just lowering his smoking rifle. His face was carved of the same caprock as the Llano Estacado. "You ain't raisin' hair on that chil', you skunkfuckin' termites!" Hudson roared. "Not while this ol' hoss's got blood and balls!"

Hudson had known, of course, there would be only one result of Whirling Storm's action. He had no problem with that, understanding as he did how Whirling Storm wanted a brave death. But it'd be a cold day in hell before he would allow some Comanche to peel his friend's scalp and leave his spirit wandering for all eternity.

The other Comanches near Whirling Storm's body backed off some, but those who were waiting beyond that shouted imprecations at Hudson and exhorted their companions. A few of the waiting Comanches began edging up. Then one ran out on foot, heading for Whirling Storm's body.

Enraged, Hudson dropped his rifle and raced forward, jerking out his two five-shot revolvers and firing.

Mad Buffalo was only a moment behind. The painted Cheyenne ran, screeching and howling, firing arrows.

Lowell, feeling like a complete and utter fool, looked at the two soldiers standing nearby. He jerked out his sword. "Charge, goddammit!" he shouted before running, neither knowing nor caring whether his men were following him.

The soldiers' efforts were not needed. Hudson and Mad Buffalo had, between the two of them in their ferocity, driven the remaining Comanches from the battlefield and back toward their village.

Hudson stopped and stood there, chest rising and falling. He looked around, saw Lowell and two soldiers trotting up. While he knew it had been of no use, he still respected Lowell for charging along with him and Mad Buffalo. "How big was that village?" Hudson asked the Cheyenne.

"Twelve, maybe fifteen lodges."

Hudson nodded. "I'll take Whirling Storm's body back to the camp. You prowl around and keep an eye out for Comanches, though I don't think they'll be back."

"I have other things to do, too," Mad Buffalo said seriously.

"I know," Hudson said quietly. "Just don't let that get in the way of what's got to be done. That might be a small village, but there's got to be other bands around. We need to make some plans."

Mad Buffalo nodded and turned. He began gathering arrows as Hudson shoved his pistols away. Then Hudson picked up Whirling Storm's corpse in his arms. "Let's git on back to camp, Sergeant," he said.

"There's nothin' we can do here?" Lowell asked.

"Nope. Not unless you want to watch Mad Buffalo's handiwork with those Comanches layin' there."

"I think not," Lowell said seriously. He sighed. God, he thought, what blood had been shed here today. He was not sure he was prepared for this. He had never thought things would be this bad. So much blood and exposed body parts. It was not the relatively clean and neat warfare he expected, had been taught to expect. "All right, men," he finally said, looking at the two disheveled soldiers who had followed him into battle, "let's get back to the camp. There's plenty of work to be done."

Darkness fell soon. Under its barely comforting cover, Hudson's men hastily helped their wounded onto horses and put Whirling Storm's body on his pony. Then they moved off hard and fast, slowing only after they had been on the trail an hour or two.

Somewhere, sometime during the night, not many hours before dawn, Hudson called a short halt. He and Mad Buffalo conferred for a few minutes in Cheyenne. Then Mad Buffalo pulled out, towing

Whirling Storm's body on the pony behind him. Hudson got the others moving again, still heading northwestward.

"Where's Mad Buffalo going?" Lowell asked as they rode on.

"We know of a spot where he can bury Whirlin' Storm so his body won't be found. I'll be damned if I'm gonna let the goddamn Comanches or some wild animals fuck up Whirlin' Storm's journey to the spirit world."

As dawn began coloring the sky, Hudson pulled them into a wooded spot along another creek bed. There was some water in the creek, though not much. The banks were not too steep in this section but were covered by brush. Several cottonwoods and a few smaller trees offered some protection from the rising sun.

"Have your boys get some sleep, Sergeant," Hudson said as he dismounted and then tied off his pony.

"What about the horses and all?"

"Hell with 'em for the time bein'."

"Keepin' watch?"

"I'll see to it."

Lowell couldn't find it in himself to argue, though he wanted to volunteer to keep watch. Trouble was, he knew he'd not be able to keep awake more than a few minutes. He didn't know how Hudson could still be so alert, after all the travel, the worry, the loss of his friend, the fighting, his wounds. Lowell felt like less than a man as he stretched out on his bedroll.

Hudson let them have a few hours of uneasy sleep before he woke them all. By then, Mad Buffalo had returned and Stolen Back Woman had made coffee and food. The hot meal and the hotter sunlight served to revive their spirits a little.

In the light of the day, they checked their wounded. No one was too bad off, and between Hudson, Lowell, and Stolen Back Woman, they got their wounds patched up and poulticed. Then they sat for a council of war.

"I think we should head back," Private Tommy McKagan said straight off.

"You that scared?" Hudson asked harshly. He was tired, his eyes rimmed with red, and he was nursing a newborn hatred for Comanches. Because of it all, he was in poor humor.

"Hell, yes," McKagan said. "Ain't you other boys?" Most nodded.

Hudson partly turned and pointed over his shoulder. "Bent's place is back that way," he said flatly. "It'll take you a week, maybe a little less if you push it some."

"Now, just wait a minute, Mister Hudson," Lowell said stiffly. "I think we might have to give some consideration to turnin' back." He paused. "I ain't sayin' we should turn back. Just that we might have to consider it."

"Why?" Hudson asked harshly.

"Well, Mister Hudson, it's ..."

"It's still Linus, Sergeant. Jist because we disagree or have differences don't mean we cain't be civil or still be friends."

That surprised Lowell a little. At least the part about being friends. He liked Hudson and would've been proud to consider the former mountain man a friend. He just hadn't considered that Hudson would allow it. He nodded, though, covering over his surprise. "Well, Linus, it's pretty damn obvious we can't just walk into whatever Comanche village we find and ask if the men—and women—are there. Maybe we could've once. That's why Mad Buffalo and Whirling Storm came with us. Or so you said. But that's certainly not an option now."

Lowell paused, thinking. Then he added, "Hell, we still don't even have any idea where they are, let alone how we're gonna get 'em back."

"So, goin' back and tellin' Kearny we was whupped is gonna solve the problem, eh?" Hudson said somewhat sarcastically.

Lowell shook his head at the foolishness of it. "Reckon that wouldn't work, would it?"

"Nope."

Lowell nodded, "Then we go on like we were before?"

"To some degree. What we need to do is go about findin' Comanche villages. That ain't gonna be as easy as it might seem either."

"No, I don't think it will," Lowell agreed. He had seen this country for more than a week now; had traveled through it, seen its emptiness. While Comanches, or any other Indians, could seem to be mighty populous when they were coming at you in a fight, finding a village of them seemed to be a considerably more forlorn proposition.

"Suppose we do find the village where they're being held?" Lowell asked. He was beginning to think that highly unlikely.

"Then we'll have to use stealth or force, whichever seems best at the time, to get them boys out of there."

"What're our chances?"

"Somewhere between none and a lot less than that," Hudson said honestly. "And the longer the time is from their havin' been taken, the harder it's gonna be to find 'em."

"I figure, too," Lowell said more than asked, "that the more time we spend in lookin' also lessens the likelihood that they'll be alive anyway?"

"The soldiers, yes. They might keep the women and adopt 'em into the band. They do that a lot with Mexicans."

"While Mister Bent might be concerned about the women," Lowell said stiffly, "I'm not. My mission is to get back those Dragoons."

"I know that," Hudson said evenly. "I'm jist tellin' you what the chances are of findin' 'em or of 'em bein' alive."

Lowell almost smiled. "Seems another reason for turnin' back, don't it?" he muttered.

"I told you that right from the get-go, boy," Hudson said. He had believed then that they should have just turned back. Now he didn't want to. Whether it was revenge for Whirling Storm's death or just not wanting to return without giving it a fair shot, he didn't know. All he knew was that he was not about to turn back just yet.

"Then we press on?" Lowell asked.

"Yep."

Lowell nodded.

"Ah, for chrissakes, Sarge," McKagan muttered, "this is bullshit. We ain't gonna find those boys. Not in another week. Not in another year. What in hell do we have to go roamin' around out here in this heat for, just sittin' ducks for some crazy goddamn Comanches."

"Tommy's right," Farmer said in a measured voice. He still feared Hudson and Mad Buffalo and didn't want to incite them unnecessarily. All he wanted to do was get back to the protection of the army. Then he would plot his revenge against the two of them. Once he had a bunch of friends with him, taking the Cheyenne and the former mountain man would not be a problem. "Let's just go back and tell Kearny we couldn't find 'em. He'll understand that. If he don't, tough shit. Let him send some others out this way. They'll find out you can't find shit."

"You others feel the same?" Lowell asked, feigning interest in what his patrol thought.

All but O'Murray nodded.

"That's interestin' to hear, men," Lowell said slowly. "But it don't mean a damn thing."

"Why the hell not?" Farmer demanded.

"It's simple, boys," Lowell said, almost elated that he had thought of this. "Put yourself in their position. You've been captured by hostile Comanches and dragged off to God knows where. And the army sends out a patrol to rescue you, but as soon as times get a little hard, the patrol turns tail and runs."

"I'd not like that, Gott im Himmel," Hochner said with vehemence. "I vould vant those boys to keep lookink for me."

The others agreed.

"Go see to your chores, boys," Lowell finally said, once it was clear that their decision had been made. "Then you best get some sleep. We'll need to push even harder now. The trail's growin' colder every minute."

As the soldiers drifted away, Hudson looked at Lowell and grinned. "I ain't sure I like the results, but you showed some gumption there, boy. That was one hell of a way to turn the tide against runnin'."

Lowell flushed in pride, but he shrugged. "As odd as it might sound, Linus, it's true, though. Every time I think of turnin' back, I think for a minute of what it'd be like to be a captive of those savages."

"Well, it worked. I just hope we don't live to regret it." Hudson chuckled a little.

When they were alone, Mad Buffalo asked Hudson in Cheyenne, "There's something I want to tell you, my friend. Is now the time?"

"Does it have anything to do with this task we're on?" Hudson countered. They were speaking in Cheyenne, so none of the others, except Stolen Back Woman, could understand them.

Mad Buffalo nodded. He did not like having to do this. He would much rather deal with it himself but that would not do in such a situation. Not when it involved the dealings of the white men with each other.

"Tell it," Hudson said. He was sure he was not going to like this.

"The blue coat who pissed his pants ..." Mad Buffalo said.

"Farmer?" Hudson questioned.

Mad Buffalo nodded. "He did no fighting in the battle with the Comanches."

"He didn't?" Hudson was more surprised than anything.

Mad Buffalo shook his head. "I watched him sometimes," the Cheyenne said. "He either hid his face, or he pretended to shoot at them." He spit in contempt. "He's a coward. I should've killed him when I had the chance."

Hudson nodded. "Maybe you should've, my friend. Might've saved us all a lot of trouble." He paused. "But it's too late for that now. We need all the men we have if we're to find those other soldiers."

"Do you think we will?" Mad Buffalo asked skeptically.

Hudson shook his head.

"Me either." Mad Buffalo paused. "What about the blue coat who pissed his pants?"

"I'll remember what you told me and I'll watch him more closely next time."

Mad Buffalo nodded. "One thing, though, my friend ... ?"

"What's that?"

"When the time comes to send that blue coat to the other world, I'd like to be the one who does it."

"So would I, old friend. So would I."

CHAPTER 12

The small group turned south. Hudson wanted to put some distance between them and the Canadian River since that was where the Comanches would be likely to have their camps. There and along the other, smaller waterways, such as there were out here.

There was almost no danger of them riding into a Comanche village by mistake. The signs that one was nearby usually could be seen for miles, unless it was a new camp. Still, even then they would have some warning before reaching it.

The main problem was the sheer vastness and emptiness of the land. They could ride for a hundred miles without seeing a Comanche camp and the trail they might want to follow had grown cold in more than a week.

The weather did not help. The heat was staggering and it showed little indication of letting up any time soon. The blazing rays of the sun hammered down on the travelers, sucking life's vital fluids up out of their pores. Their tongues swelled, and their mouths and eyes dried out. Waves of heat shimmered in the distances, making the men, especially those unused to being out in this vast openness, see things that were not really there. Interesting things, sometimes intriguing things, and often frightening things. It made the men think they had entered another world, one in which they did not belong, and in which they could not be a full part. Not that any of them wanted to be part of such a strange world.

They got rain only once but when it came it was a roaring, pounding storm that battered man and animal alike for the better part of a day. Caught in the open, and afraid to move to any lower-lying land where there might be shelter, the group plodded along, fighting the raging wind, the downpour and the frightened, struggling animals. When the storm had passed, they were a beaten, battered group of people and took two days to throw off the effects Mother Nature's rampage.

During that time, they talked much on what they should do. For the first time, Sergeant Lowell began leaning toward the idea of heading back.

"This is becomin' goddamn futile, Linus," Lowell said as he and Hudson sat around a dismal fire in a muck-sloppy camp. Though the rain had stopped the day before, water still dripped from the brush and the few trees that grew along the newly rushing creek below them down a steep bank.

Hudson shrugged. He had reason to continue the quest. It had nothing to do with the army or the soldiers who had been taken or even the women who had been captured. He doubted any of them were still alive anyway. Nor did his desire to push on have anything to do with any possible debt he owed to Bill Bent or with his having promised the army that he would do this job. No, what drove him was the simple desire for revenge, that was all. Revenge against the Comanches for having killed Whirling Storm, and for their having taken the soldiers and women, which had led in the end to the useless murder of his friend. And he wanted retribution against the Comanches for their having made him turn tail and run.

Trouble was, he could not admit any of that to Lowell. Nor could he reasonably expect Lowell to want to continue on for such a personal—to Hudson—reason. No, he would have to find some other, more plausible reason; one that Lowell could accept.

"Don't you agree?" Lowell pressed.

"I agree it's been a waste of goddamn time so far, but somethin' about turnin' back jist frosts my ass," Hudson snapped. He quieted, thinking about it. "Part of it, though," he finally said lamely, "is because I owe Bill Bent a mighty powerful lot." He almost cursed himself silently for the foolish statement.

"Mister Bent?"

"Yep. He's been mighty good to me, and from all I heard, the army's treated him like shit since they started gittin' to the fort." He knew the story was going downhill in a hurry.

"The fortunes of war," Lowell said with a fatalistic shrug.

Hudson nodded. "I know, but still, he's seen me

through some hard times. I'd like to be able to pay him back a little by findin' them women for him. Still, that ain't much of a reason."

"Well," Lowell said into the breach of silence that had grown, "much as I hate to say it, I've got to agree that ain't enough reason for goin' on." He paused, then added, "Hell, Linus, we don't even know where to look for 'em anymore."

"Maybe we do," Hudson said thoughtfully. He put the other matter in the back of his mind for the moment.

"Where?" Lowell asked suspiciously.

Hudson pointed northeast. "Back that way. Beyond that village that sent those warriors after us."

"Why?"

Hudson shook his head, annoyed at himself for not having seen this right from the start. "Hell, every sign we saw of those boys who took your friends was movin' in that direction. Goddammit, those soldiers had to have been in that goddamn camp. If they're alive." He paused. "They might've moved on already, but that war party had to have stayed there at least a little."

"What makes you say that?" Lowell was interested and thought Hudson might be on to something here.

"That camp was the first place we saw any real recent sign of any Comanches other than that war party," Hudson offered, still thinking it through as he talked. "Comanches often raid a place, then ride like hell for a day or two to put as much distance between them and any possible pursuit as they can."

"So?"

"So, they rode like hell for a couple of days, slowed down a little, and then found the first village of friends. They'd be sure as shit to stop there and have themselves some doin's to celebrate their 'victory' over the army. They would've had their friends help 'em treat those soldier boys rough for some entertainment and they would've sported considerable with the women."

"I think Linus's right," Mad Buffalo said with a firm nod. "That's just the way those damned Comanches would've acted." He spit in disgust, even though he and his men most likely would've done exactly the same had they been the ones to make captives of the soldiers and the women. Still, he was angry at the Comanches for his and Whirling Storm's treatment at their hands and he could no longer consider any Comanche a friend.

Lowell thought that over for a bit. He knew almost nothing about Indians; all he knew was what he had learned on this short trip. However, his instincts—and stories he had heard back in the States—led him to believe that Hudson was on the right track. It made a lot of sense as best he could figure it.

"So," Lowell said, "what do we do? Just ride back to that village and storm it?"

Hudson gave him a withering look. "You see any sign them boys—or the women—was in that village, Mad Buffler?" he asked, looking at his longtime friend.

The Cheyenne shook his head, his hair flying about. "Couldn't tell about the women. There was a few looked like they were Mexican captives runnin' about. Could've been them. Or others. But if them soldiers was there, they was hid good. I didn't even git a whiff of 'em."

Hudson nodded. "I figure they were gone. Again, if they're still alive."

"You think they are?" Lowell asked. "Alive, I mean."

Hudson shrugged. "Beats the shit out of me. There's no reason for the Comanches to kill 'em, unless those boys've caused too much trouble. There are a couple reasons to keep 'em alive."

"Such as?" Lowell asked, surprised.

"Could be as simple as them wantin' to spread the amusements 'round amongst as many of their people as they can. Could be that they want to keep 'em as slaves of a sort. They do that plenty with Mexican men and boys they take. Of course, it helps if the captives're a heap younger. Then they'll eventually adopt 'em into the band. Hell, a couple years out in the Llano with a band of Comanches and any young'n'll forget what he really is underneath."

"Those reasons don't sound real convincin', Linus."

Hudson grinned without humor, but a brainstorm had hit him. "That's a fact, boy," he growled as he tossed out the dregs of his coffee, mind working up the story. "But there might be a more compellin' reason—ransomin' them."

"The army'd never pay a ransom," Lowell said. He took another piece of buffalo meat from the fire and chewed it.

"It ain't the army I'm talkin' about. It's the Mexicans."

"What the hell would the Mexicans ransom a couple of American soldiers for? Jesus, Linus, we're at war with Mexico."

"Jist think, boy," Hudson said slowly. He hadn't fully thought this out either, but he was beginning to warm up to the task. "What use could Governor Armijo—who's head of all the Mexicans in these parts—make of a couple of captured American soldiers?"

Lowell shrugged. "Try'n trade 'em back for maybe some favors from Colonel Kearny?"

"Shit, boy," Hudson snorted. "Kearny'd never go for somethin' like that. Not for a couple of lowly soldiers. A few officers, maybe, but even then I doubt it. But a couple soldiers in Armijo's hands could go a long way toward convincin' a wary citizenry that he's somethin' special."

"He's already the governor, you said."

"Don't mean the people like him any. Hell, you like every goddamn shitstick politician, bureaucrat, and official you have to deal with?"

"Well, no, but... "

"But shit. I'd wager that more'n half the Mexicans in northern Mexico hate that son of a bitch. About the only support he's got is from the ricos—the rich folk. But if he had himself a couple American soldiers captive, he could go to the peons and show them blue coats around with dire warnin's about what his people'll face when the Americans git to Taos and Santa Fe. He can also brag about how his men maybe defeated a big force of Americans and took these ones prisoners. That'd make him look pretty good in the eyes of the Mexicans."

"But that's not true," Lowell protested, knowing even as he said it that he was being a fool.

"Christ, boy," Hudson snorted. "We're talkin' about a bunch of uneducated, ignorant, superstitious, goddamn Mexican peons here. They don't know but from what they can see or what Armijo tells 'em. He says ten thousand Americans are marchin' on Taos and shows off a couple captives, they got no choice but to believe him."

Lowell nodded slowly, absorbing it. It was entirely plausible, he decided. He did not know the Mexican people, but if his own countrymen were any indication, the Mexicans would be as gullible as anyone else. He had seen how two ragged, poor-devil Indians stealing a couple of chickens could result in the countryside being inflamed by the fear of some major Indian uprising. Still, something didn't seem right about it. He snapped his fingers, as it came to him.

"What about the Comanches?" he asked. "Why would they trade the captives to the Mexicans? Didn't you say they were enemies with Mexico?"

"Hell, the Comanches're enemies with everybody. Don't stop 'em from dealin' with anyone when they're of a mind to. They've been sellin' captives back to the Mexicans for years. The Mexican officials're too goddamn stupid to see that they're bein' used. And don't be fooled, boy. Jist 'cause the Comanches live out here in the back ass of nowhere don't mean they don't know what's goin' on. They know there's big trouble between the Americans and the Mexicans."

"So?" Lowell was confused. There had been too much information in too short a time and all about people of which he knew absolutely nothing.

"The Comanches might be uneducated people, Sergeant," Hudson said quietly. "That don't mean they're ignorant. When it comes to war and all its intrigues, these boys are amongst the best. They can see what might happen if they ransomed a couple American soldiers to the Mexicans. For one thing, it'd keep the Mexicans off their backs for a while, possibly. But more importantly, it'd go a long way toward keepin' the Mexicans and Americans mad at each other for a while. The Comanches jist might figure that those two armies'll kill each other off nice and neat and then Comancheria will be theirs again."

"Goddamn, that's diabolical," Lowell said. "If it's true," he added pointedly. He found it hard to believe that such a savage and simple people as any Indian tribe could conceive of such a plan, much less execute it. But Hudson seemed so sure of it.

Hudson shrugged. "I ain't sayin' it's true, Sergeant," he said smoothly. "But I know the Comanches're capable of such a thing and it would work out to their advantage. Not that they would've thought such a thing right from the start, mind you. A couple of them boys might've been headin' to Bent's to trade, found the soldiers and the women and took 'em captive since that's their nature. They might've rid to that village with the idea of sportin' with 'em all and then had some of the elders, some of 'em with sense instead of hot blood, come up with such a plan."

Lowell's head spun with it all. Finally, he shook his head, trying to clear it of some of the befuddlement. It didn't work. "I've got to sleep on all this, Linus," he said, pushing himself up. "Try'n sort it all out in my mind."

Hudson nodded. He knew Lowell would not be able to sleep at all but he could do nothing about that. He didn't feel particularly good about going through all this, leading Lowell on, as it were, though such a thing was a possibility. Still, he felt strongly enough about his desire for avenging Whirling Storm to tell Lowell anything for the moment.

"You think any of that shit's true, Fierce Bear?" Mad Buffalo asked skeptically when Lowell had left.

"I doubt it," Hudson admitted. "But Lowell don't know that and it damn well could be. Hell, the Comanches've been jerkin' the goddamn Mexicans around for years with their deceits and whatnot. I don't know as if they could reason this out but if they think about it at all, they've got to know there's a good chance they can raise all kinds of ruckus between the two sides by playin' such a game. The trick is gettin' both sides to take the bait." He grinned a little. "And we both know what kind of gamblers all you red devils are."

Mad Buffalo laughed softly. "Almost as big gamblers as you white eyes," he agreed. Then he grew serious again. "Why'd you tell him all that shit then?" he asked.

"I aim to pay some Comanches back for killin'

Whirlin' Storm," Hudson said bluntly.

Mad Buffalo nodded and smiled grimly in the darkness. "So I had hoped, my friend," he said quietly.

"I don't know how plausible any of that shit you told me last night is, Linus," Lowell said as he sat and accepted a cup of morning coffee from Stolen Back Woman. "But it sure as hell makes sense. I'll be angrier'n all hell was you to be pullin' my leg on this but I don't think you are." He looked questioningly at Hudson.

"I ain't pullin' your leg, boy. I got no idea if I'm foolin' myself with all this nonsense but it's an idea I think the Comanches're capable of." He paused, then added, "Of course, if that's not convincin' enough for you, you might want to consider what Kearny'll say if we go back without the soldiers— or without payin' back the Comanches for havin' taken them to begin with."

"He wouldn't be pleased," Lowell agreed.

"I figure not. Especially without a payback. That's all Kearny needs is thinkin', he's got the Mexican army out front of him and a heap of willful Comanches ridin' up his ass."

Lowell nodded, suddenly looking worried. "I reckon we do have reason to keep lookin' for them, don't we?"

Hudson laughed a little. It took a minute but then Lowell joined him.

CHAPTER 13

"Won't those Comanches be headin' this way if they plan to try to ransom our soldiers in Taos, Linus?" Lowell asked as they were downing their morning meal.

"Eventually." Hudson could still not believe that Lowell was buying the story, despite its ring of truth. "But it don't mean they have to come right past this here exact spot. Nor does it mean they're fixin' to do that straight off."

"So we head back toward that village?"

"Yep." Hudson tossed the last of his coffee out and stood. "We should be able to cut some sign of them blue coats there. Now, let's git a move on, boy."

They headed northeast, making better time than they had in a spell. While there was some worry about what they were heading into, most of the men seemed eager to see some kind of action rather than just plodding through the flat, desolate country.

It took them just over a day and a half to make it back to the area where they had had the battle with the Comanches. They stopped well before they got there, though it seemed as if the Comanche camp had moved on, at least from a distance. While the soldiers made camp, Hudson and Mad Buffalo rode off to scout out the area. The two were gone until well after dark.

Hudson and Mad Buffalo moved back into the camp so silently that Private Halsey Butterworth, who was assigned to guard the horses, never heard them. Even the horses themselves showed little sign of agitation when the two men slipped among them with their own horses. It was only after Hudson had dropped his saddle softly on the ground with a muffled thump that Butterworth knew someone was around.

"Who's there?" he whispered, fear in his voice.

"Who the hell you think, boy?" Hudson responded from just behind Butterworth. He was surprised that the soldier didn't fire off his rifle by accident when he jumped at Hudson's voice.

"Goddamn, Mister Hudson," he said softly, "where'd you come from? You scared the living shit out of me."

"A good lesson to remember, boy," Hudson said easily. "The Comanches wouldn't be so polite."

"Yessir." Butterworth went back to patrolling around the horses. He was almost sick with disgust at having failed at his post and with the fear of wondering what would have happened if that had really been Comanches instead of Hudson and Mad Buffalo. He vowed to be more alert, or at least try to be.

Hudson headed silently toward where Stolen Back Woman had been putting their little camp within the larger camp. As he neared the site, he thought he heard ragged breathing, and he tensed a little. He began moving more cautiously. Then he stopped and smiled grimly. In the pale, dim glow of the small fire's embers, he could see Stolen Back Woman sitting on their buffalo robes, her own .36-caliber Colt Paterson revolver in her hand. The pistol was cocked and pointed at the chest of Private Gregg Farmer.

"You best put that goddamn gun away, missy," Farmer was saying, "before someone gets hurt. And that's most likely gonna be you."

Hudson was about to step forward, but he decided to wait a bit, to see what else Farmer might have to say. He didn't have long to wait.

"Now I'm gettin' mighty tired of this game, missy," Farmer said, voice irritated. "You know damn well your ol' man ain't comin' back. Him and that shitlickin' Cheyenne friend of yours have gone off by themselves, leavin' us here at the mercy of them damned Comanches out yonder. Now, I'd be willin' to give you some protection from them red devils was you to start treatin' me nice. I mean, I come over here offerin' you my friendship and comfort and ..."

Hudson had heard about enough. Rage simmered in his veins and he wanted to just shoot Farmer in the head here and now and be done with it. But they would need all their guns, especially if they confronted the Comanches again, which Hudson had every intention of doing. He set his rifle down and moved forward, as silent and deadly as a cougar, drawing his knife as he walked. Suddenly he knelt behind Farmer, who still had no idea Hudson was there, grabbed him around the throat and with one easy movement, sliced off Farmer's right ear.

Farmer let out a squawk that was quickly clamped off by Hudson's powerful right hand.

"You get within a dozen feet of my woman again, shit stick and I'll cut you dick off and shove it up your ass," Hudson growled. "You got that?"

Farmer mumbled something. Hudson eased the pressure on the soldier's throat and Farmer hissed, "I'll gut you for this, you son of a bitch. I'll..." He reached up and touched the side of his head for the first time. "Jesus fuckin' Christ, you cut off my ear, goddammit!" Hudson screeched.

"Jist remember what I said," Hudson said as he wiped his knife off on the back of Farmer's uniform.

The other soldiers, led by Sergeant Lowell were moving up swiftly even as Hudson stood and slid his knife away.

"What the hell's all the noise about?" Lowell asked gruffly, voice still ragged with the edges of sleep. He held a small torch up.

Farmer jumped up and pointed at Hudson. "That crazy bastard just up and cut my goddamn ear off!" he shouted. "For no goddamn reason." He suddenly dropped to his knees and began frantically patting the ground, looking for his missing appendage.

"That true, Linus?" Lowell asked, surprised.

"First part is," Hudson said easily. "The part about whackin' off his ear. The other part ain't right, though. I had me a goddamn good reason."

"Which was?" Lowell didn't know what to think.

"Suppose you ask shit stick."

"Private?" Lowell questioned.

"Go to hell," Farmer said, continuing his desperate search. "I got to find my ear. We can sew it back on."

"Answer me, Private!" Lowell roared. He had been feeling out of place ever since he had started on this mission and he just now had decided that it was time to reassert himself and his authority. "Or I'll cut off the other goddamn ear."

Farmer stopped scrabbling in the dark dirt and looked up. When he saw the look on Lowell's face, he rose slowly. "No goddamn reason, Sergeant," he said unctuously. "I couldn't sleep and I was just settin' there talkin' with the woman when all of a sudden this asshole lops off my ear."

"That what happened, Linus?" Lowell asked. He was quite certain Farmer was lying.

"Not the way I saw it."

Lowell glared at Farmer a moment, then looked at Stolen Back Woman and smiled a little. "What did happen, ma'am?" he asked quietly.

"Blue coat tried to ... to ..." She stumbled to a halt. It wasn't that she was embarrassed by trying to say that Farmer had attempted to force himself on her; it was just that she didn't have the command of English to be able to tell it.

Lowell didn't know that, of course, and hastily asked, "He tried to have his way with you against your will? Was that it, ma'am?" He paused a second. "Sorry, but I have to ask."

Stolen Back Woman nodded, unabashed. "Yes," she said. "Yes, that's what he do. Try to do. But I have a gun. Fierce Bear give to me. I can use."

"I just bet you can," Lowell said dryly. "So you managed to get your pistol out and get him to back off?"

"Yes. It happen that way," Stolen Back Woman said with a firm nod. "I tell him wait here till Fierce Bear come back."

"I found her sittin' holdin' her pistol on him, Sergeant," Hudson said. "I overheard him tryin' to tell her that me and Mad Buffalo had gone off and left y'all. Goddamn idiot."

It took Lowell some moments before he could bring his anger under control enough to enable him to speak. When he did, it was with hard, cold tones. "I didn't think even an asshole like you could stoop so low, Private. Your behavior is of the basest sort and is reprehensible. By rights, I ought to shoot you dead right here and now. The army'd agree with me, too. Trouble is, I really can't afford to do that now."

Farmer smirked. He had known Lowell wouldn't risk killing him. All hands were needed against the Comanches, for one thing. Besides, though Farmer knew Lowell didn't like him, they were still army compatriots, and he didn't think Lowell had it in him to kill anyone, much less a fellow soldier.

"But let me warn you, Private," Lowell continued icily. "If you make it back to Bent's Fort alive, you'll regret what you tried to do here tonight."

The smirk began fading from Farmer's face but he was still not too worried. He figured that by the time they got back to Bent's, he could worm himself back into the army's good graces, if not Lowell's. Kearny would never allow one of his troops to be disciplined because of something that almost happened, but didn't, to an Indian woman.

"And, lest you think I've gone soft," Lowell added, "heed this. Do something like this again and you will die then and there. By my hand or Mister Hudson's." Without looking away from Farmer, he said, "Private O'Murray, relieve Private Farmer of his sidearm and other weapons. You'll get 'em back when we're under attack and not before, Farmer. And for the rest of the night you'll be under Private Hochner's watch."

Hudson waited until the soldiers were gone before going to get his rifle. Then he sat on the robes while Stolen Back Woman served him some food and coffee. Once he was eating, he asked, "You all right, woman?"

Stolen Back Woman nodded. She smiled shyly at her husband.

"He didn't do nothin' to you?"

"No." She paused, worried. "If he had, you wouldn't love me anymore?"

"You know better'n that," Hudson said quietly. "But if he had done somethin' to you, he wouldn't live out the night."

"He did nothing." She almost laughed. "It was almost funny," she said in Cheyenne. "He thought he was the big man. Oh, so strong and wonderful. So he thought." She could not contain a few giggles. "He boasted of how much of a man he was and how this ignorant Cheyenne girl could use a man of his experience." She covered her smooth, full mouth with a small, brown hand as if trying to squelch laughter. If she was so trying, she was having little success.

"And I suppose you believed every word of it, yes?" Hudson said with a grin.

"Oh, yes," Stolen Back Woman said, laughter rippling out of her smiling moon face regularly now. "I almost fainted at his strength and power. Flat on my back I went, helpless under the assault of his manliness." Tears of mirth were leaking from her eyes now. "I could see the hunger in him then, as he began to reach for what he wanted so much. And just as his fingers were about to touch that spot..." She laughed harder and lifted one hand, making a pistol out of it, "I surprised him."

"About shit his pants, did he?" Hudson asked, laughing with Stolen Back Woman.

"Oh, yes! You should have seen his face. Angry and frightened and annoyed all at one time. His mouth flapped around with no sounds coming out. His eyes were like an owl's, so big and round. I told him to sit back and we would wait for you."

"How long did you have to wait?" Hudson asked, touching Stolen Back Woman's face gently with a grimy, callused forefinger.

"Not too long. An hour maybe."

"And all the while he was trying to get you to put the gun down so he could jump on you?"

Stolen Back Woman nodded and finally stopped laughing. With wide, serious eyes, she looked at Hudson. "I wanted to shoot him anyway," she said quietly. "Just for trying."

"Nothin' wrong in that, woman. It wouldn't've been such a bad thing if you'd gone ahead and done it."

"I was afraid the blue coat chief would hurt me if I killed one of his men."

"Sergeant Lowell? I doubt it. He didn't much like Farmer anyway. He would've believed you if you had told him what happened." Hudson was sure of that beyond any doubt. He considered himself a fairly good judge of men and he liked what he had seen of Sergeant Alfred Lowell.

"You think so?"

Hudson nodded and finished eating. He looked at Stolen Back Woman and smiled. "You feelin' good enough to let a real man have a go at you, woman?" he asked huskily, wanting her badly.

"Oh, I don't know," she teased in Cheyenne. "After such a manly man as the blue coat, I'm not sure."

"Shit," Hudson breathed as he reached for her. Laughing, the two tumbled down onto the robes.

"May I sit, Linus?" Lowell asked in the morning. He was embarrassed.

"Suit yourself." Hudson looked askance at the soldier. "Somethin' wrong with you, boy?" he asked.

"I'm ... Well, goddammit, I'm nearabout mortified at what happened last night. I half thought you'd be angry at me since it was one of my men tried such a heinous thing. And I wouldn't blame you at all for bein' mad."

"I don't harbor no hard feelin's for you, Sergeant," Hudson said honestly. "You had no control of what that dickless oaf did. And when you learned of it, you handled it the best that could be done. Don't you go worryin' none over it. Coffee?"

"Thanks," Lowell said, relieved. He took the cup from Stolen Back Woman but he still could not look at her. Not yet.

He did look at her, though, and even managed a little smile when she touched his cheek with a finger and said softly, "You're good man. I like you."

Lowell shook his head in wonder and glanced out of the corner of his eye at Hudson. The former mountain man could barely contain a grin at Lowell's discomfiture. Linus took a few sips of hot coffee and then asked, "So, what did you and Mad Buffalo learn out there yesterday?"

"We found certain sign that the soldiers were here, but it was at least several days ago. With the time that's passed, and that rain we had the other day, a lot of sign was washed out, but there was still some to read. It looks like the war party took the captives and headed northeast."

"That don't seem right, does it?"

Hudson shrugged. "They jist might be headin' back to their own village somewhere before figurin' out what to do with their prisoners. The village picked up and headed south, which ain't unusual."

"So we go northeast?"

"Yep."

"How far ahead of us are they?"

"Three, four days."

"Can we catch 'em?"

"I reckon so. We can move pretty fast and they won't be."

"Why not?"

"Got no reason to. They figure they sent us packin' after that set-to we had with 'em. And there ain't no other white men out here that I'm aware of."

Lowell nodded. "Reckon we better get movin' then." He set down his cup, stood and turned to walk away. He turned back when Hudson called him.

"You might want to give this to Farmer," Hudson said. He threw something at Lowell.

The sergeant caught it, looked down and grimaced. "It ain't gonna do him much good now," he said, gingerly holding up Farmer's dirt-covered ear. Then he grinned. "But I'll see if he wants it for a keepsake."

CHAPTER 14

They moved north and east as fast as they dared. As had become usual, Mad Buffalo rode a fair distance out front of the small group, ranging from side to side in an arc ahead of the band, always looking for sign of the Comanches.

The soldiers complained little now; except for Sergeant Alfred Lowell, they were too frightened, not sure what Hudson would do to them if they caused any sort of a ruckus. Truth to tell, though, all of them but Farmer and his only friend here, Private Tommy McKagan, were decent men who simply wanted to do their job and then get out of this hellacious country.

About midway through the next day, Mad Buffalo suddenly came racing back toward the small column. Hudson and Lowell, who were leading the group, as they normally did, stopped and called for the rest of the men to halt.

In moments, Mad Buffalo had come pounding up and jerked his pony to a standstill.

"You saw Comanches?" Hudson asked.

Mad Buffalo shook his head vigorously, his long, loose, black hair whipping back and forth. He had given up wearing his buffalohorn war hat early on. "Mexicans," he growled.

"Mexicans?" Hudson asked, surprised. "Out here?"

Mad Buffalo nodded. "Soldiers."

"How many of 'em, and where the hell are they?" Hudson asked urgently. Mad Buffalo wouldn't have come racing back here the way he had if the danger wasn't imminent.

"Couple dozen or so. Maybe three miles that way." He pointed slightly southeast. "They're movin' northwest," he added pointedly, meaning that they would run right into the small group if both bands continued the way they were going.

"They see you?" Hudson asked.

Mad Buffalo shrugged, uncertain. It made him annoyed with himself since he should have been sure not only that he knew the answer but that they hadn't seen him.

Hudson sucked in a deep breath and then eased it out. Standing in his stirrups, he looked around. The land was basically flat and completely empty as far as the eye could see. The only cover of any kind was the small folds of land as it rolled gently off to the heat-wave distorted horizon.

"They might not spot us," Hudson said to no one in particular as he settled back into his saddle. "But we cain't be sure of that." He looked at Mad Buffalo. "You got any ideas on where to go?" Hudson asked.

The Cheyenne jerked his chin, vaguely indicating

northeast. "Couple miles," he said in English. "Where those two creeks come together."

Hudson thought about it a moment. "The ones the Mexicans call Punta de Agua and Rita Blanca?" he said, thinking he had it right.

Mad Buffalo nodded. "Good spot. Some water. Wood. Enough cover if we need it."

"And maybe we won't," Hudson said hopefully. "With any luck those shit sticks'll never come near us."

Mad Buffalo looked at his friend in scorn.

Hudson laughed a little. "Yeah, I know, despite all these goddamn miles of emptiness there ain't a goddamn hope they'll miss us. Well, let's ride, boys. Maybe we can at least get there early enough to dig in some."

They rode hard and within half an hour were edging up on the confluence of two small creeks. Trouble was, they could see the Mexican soldiers coming fast from their right. The Mexicans had spotted them, too, and were pushing hard to cut them off.

Hudson stopped and took a hasty look around. Punta de Agua Creek came in from the west; the Rita Blanca from almost due north and then continued about due south. Hudson's eyes swept the land on the north bank of Punta de Agua Creek and farther on. Right along the creek bank, there was plenty of brush and enough trees to offer a fair amount of cover. Beyond that, it flattened and turned grassy. The south bank was steeply sloped and there was no vegetation but the grass and a few scraggly bushes.

South of the Punta de Agua, the Rita Blanca's banks were cut deep on both east and west. North of the other creek, trees and brush lined both banks. There was more water in each creek than Hudson had figured there would be but he quickly decided that the rain several days before had filled them and even the north Texas summer had not been able to dry them up in just a few days.

"Put the horses and mules there," he said, pointing. "Out along the fringe of trees on the far side of the creek." Remembering what Mad Buffalo had said about Farmer's lack of action during the fight with the Comanches, Hudson turned to Lowell and said, "Have Farmer watch over the animals. Tell him to make sure he keeps them along the trees, not out in the flats beyond them."

Lowell nodded and gave the order. He also made sure Farmer had his rifle and pistol back.

As the soldiers began pushing the animals toward the steep bank of the creek—and the small haven on the other side—Hudson rode up alongside Farmer. "Remember, shit stick," he said harshly, "them animals get took and you'll be on foot along with the rest of us."

"Eat shit," Farmer snapped as he jerked his horse's head around and moved off.

"I'll take up a spot over there," Hudson said, pointing again. That would put him more or less at the inside of the point where the two creeks actually met. There was a large cottonwood there and plentiful brush that would protect him. "Sergeant, have your men fan out a little, a couple of 'em on the north bank of the Punta here, the others along in those trees over on the east bank of the Rita. Stolen Back Woman'll stay with me."

"What about you, Mad Buffalo?" Lowell asked after issuing his orders.

"I'll be around," the Cheyenne said enigmatically.

Lowell nodded. "Good luck, then, Mad Buffalo. And to you, too, Linus."

The three men and one woman headed to their positions. They had barely gotten there when the Mexican soldiers pulled within range of their rifles. Resting against the Cottonwood's trunk for support, Hudson dropped one straight off at about four-hundred yards, then swiftly reloaded.

He fired again, dropping another Mexican. Then the soldiers opened fire. Two fusillades from the Americans—and one Cheyenne, who seemed to be several places at once—stopped the Mexicans cold. The soldados pulled back out of range and regrouped.

"Fuck with us, will ya, goddammit," one of the Americans shouted, pride mixed with lingering fear in his voice. "That'll show ya."

Hudson smiled, realizing Private Sean O'Murray had made the defiant statement. He looked favorably on men with bravado—as long as they could back it up and O'Murray had shown so far that he could.

The Mexicans charged again, but this time they divided into two groups and they were more spread out, riding low on their horses. One group slopped across the creek south of Hudson's position and then headed north. The other came at a right angle from the other side of the creek.

Hudson shot one more Mexican soldier off his horse but the others appeared to be unscathed. Still, the Mexicans did pull up again within a hundred yards of the Americans' position and then raced off to regroup once more.

"Shit," Hudson muttered as he ran a patch of fibrous tow through his rifle barrel a couple of times to clean it some. Then he reloaded the weapon. He quickly reloaded the fifth chamber of each of his two Colt Paterson revolvers. He shoved the pistols away and took up his rifle again, waiting and watching. His small group could not withstand many more rushes like the last one, especially if the Americans' gunfire continued to have such little effect on the soldados as it had this last time.

"Best brace yourselves, boys," Hudson called out as the Mexicans began another run for them. "I think this time those shit sticks're gonna go all out."

"Let them goddamn boys come," O'Murray shouted. "We'll kick their sorry asses!"

Hudson grinned again but then grew serious. By the time the Mexicans had covered two hundred yards, he had fired his rifle four times. Then he dropped it and yanked out his two pistols. He stepped out from behind the tree and fired them smoothly, evenly.

When they were empty, he tossed the revolvers aside and slid back behind the tree. He had no time to reload the pistols since the soldados were almost on them all now. He bent and swept up his rifle. As the Mexicans began charging into the Americans' position, he stepped out into the open again.

A Mexican's horse reared in fright at the sudden apparition. The soldier managed to keep his seat but as soon as his horse's hooves landed back on earth, Hudson stepped up and clubbed the man across the chest with his rifle. The soldier fell and the horse raced off.

When the Mexican began getting up, Hudson moved in and grabbed the man by the hair. He jerked the soldier to his feet, the yanked him forward, until the soldier's face slammed into the tree trunk. The Mexican's knees buckled, but Hudson managed to keep him mostly upright, at least long enough to smash his head into the tree again. He let the soldier fall.

Hudson was just about to plunge his big knife into the Mexican's swollen chest when Stolen Back Woman screamed. Hudson straightened but was only half turned when a sword wielded by another mounted Mexican soldier clipped the top of his head on the left side. The power of the blow spun him and knocked him down.

Groggy, and with blood streaming down the side of his face, Hudson tried to get up. He knew instinctively that the Mexican would be making another run at him any moment. He made it and staggered back a few steps until he could rest his back against the cottonwood trunk. He swiped at the blood that had poured into his left eye.

A moment later, Stolen Back Woman was there, thrusting his two Colts at him. She had reloaded them as swiftly as she could. Hudson nodded in thanks and then shoved the woman out of the way. The soldier was bearing down on him again. Hudson stood his ground and fired off three shots. All three lead balls smacked into the soldier's fat face and the man rolled off the rump of his horse. Hudson stepped up and shot the soldier in the forehead at close range, just to make sure.

Hudson stood a moment, looking over the battlefield. Gunfire still popped occasionally, but silence seemed to be spreading. Something seemed odd to him but Hudson could not figure out what with the pain in his head. Then it hit him. He jerked his head up and around and saw through the trees that the Mexicans were fleeing—with the Americans' herd of horses and mules. "Shit, goddamn," he muttered. Weary, he sank down until he was sitting.

With the help of Stolen Back Woman and Mad Buffalo, he was standing by the time Lowell and the soldiers came up and stopped uncomfortably in front of him.

"They're all gone, ain't they?" Hudson asked, voice a low growl.

Lowell nodded. "Every goddamn last one of 'em." He looked Hudson straight in the eyes, unwilling to show his fear or annoyance. "And all the goddamn supplies, too."

"Jesus," Hudson muttered.

"We're in dire straits, ain't we?" Lowell asked, stomach knotting.

"That's a brilliant fuckin' statement," Hudson responded sarcastically. He took a couple of deep breaths to calm himself down some and to try to ease the pain in his head. "Anyone hurt?" he asked.

"Private O'Murray's got a small leg wound," Lowell said. "And Private Hogg lost a finger to a bullet. That's about it. And you, of course. What the hell happened?"

Hudson explained it in a few words.

"Think they'll be back?" Lowell asked when Hudson had finished.

Hudson shook his head and immediately regretted it.

"How sure of that are you?" Lowell was considerably worried and didn't mind that anyone knew it.

"Those shiteatin' greasers're a hell of a lot more interested in our horses and supplies than they are in killin' us," Hudson answered. "Them supplies'll keep them boys goin' for a while, and that cavvyard of horses and mules'll bring 'em a pretty penny in San Miguel or somewhere. Those boys're gonna be rich by their standards. Why risk gittin' killed when you can sell some horses for good money and then spend the next six months doin' nothin but drinkin' mescal and humpin' some pretty senoritas?"

The men grew silent then, somewhat relieved but still worried as to what they would do now. All of them knew they were miles from any kind of help, and they were without food, water, and extra ammunition. In the heart of Comanche country. With Mexican soldiers still roaming around.

Mad Buffalo leaned over and whispered into Hudson's ear in Cheyenne for a minute or so. Hudson gave his Cheyenne friend a look that showed only a little surprise. Then he turned hard eyes on Farmer, who suddenly seemed to be trying to hide behind the other soldiers. "Where were you when those goddamn greasers got the horses and such?" he asked harshly.

"Tryin' to watch over 'em," Farmer answered defiantly.

"Didn't do a very goddamn good job of it, did you, shit stick?"

"Christ, Hudson, there was stinkin' Mexicans all over the goddamn place. I couldn't be everywhere at once. Even an asshole like you ought to know that."

"You wasn't such a skunksuckin' chickenshit, we'd still have them goddamn animals."

"There's no need for such talk, Linus," Lowell said sternly. "We were considerably outnumbered, and I'm sure Private Farmer did the best he could under the circumstances."

"That so?" Hudson countered sarcastically.

"I believe so," Lowell said stiffly. He had no liking for Farmer, but he didn't think he could stand by while Hudson remonstrated the soldier for no good reason.

"Why don't you ask that dickless little fart what he was doin' that time while the rest of us were tryin' to keep the goddamn Comanches from raisin' our hair?"

"Same goddamn thing you were, goddammit."

"Mad Buffler says you never fired a shot," Hudson said flatly. His anger had risen enough to almost blot out the pain in his head.

"Christ, Hudson," Farmer snorted, "you're gonna

believe the word of a fuckin' savage?"

It took a moment before Hudson was calm enough to speak. "I'd place my life in Mad Buffler's hands anywhere, anytime, boy," he growled. "As for you, I wouldn't piss down your throat if your innards were on fire. You ain't worth the sweat off Mad Buffler's balls."

"Why you Injunlovin' son of a bitch," Farmer snapped. "I'm of a good mind to carve your goddamn heart out right here and now."

"You ain't got the balls or the strength, boy," Hudson said scornfully. "You did, you would've fought the Comanches that time. And you would've made a better showin' of yourself here today."

"I ain't listenin' to no more of this old man's shit," Farmer said angrily. He turned and began to walk away.

"Front and center, Private!" Lowell roared. When a sullen Farmer came back and stood in front of Lowell, the sergeant said, "Let me see your sidearm, Private."

"What for?"

"Now!" Lowell bellowed.

Rage etching his face, Farmer pulled the single-shot pistol out of his belt and handed it butt first to Lowell.

The sergeant sniffed the muzzle, and swiftly pulled the hammer back and checked the percussion cap on the nipple. He glared at Lowell for some moments before he hissed, "Goddamn thing ain't been fired."

"I told you, Sergeant," Farmer said lamely, "I

was tendin' to the horses. I thought it was more important to make sure they didn't get away than to stand there tryin' to fire and load a single-shot pistol while two dozen goddamn Mexicans were overrunnin' our position." Sweat coated his face.

"You don't sound very convincin', Private," Lowell said tightly. "Even to yourself, I'd wager." He sighed, then ordered, "Private O'Murray, please take Private Farmer into your custody. Watch over him well till I decide what to do with him."

CHAPTER 15

"You ain't placin' me under arrest, goddammit," Farmer snapped. "Not just on the word of that asshole."

"You'll goddamn do what I say!" Lowell thundered.

"Let him be, Sergeant," Hudson said quietly.

Lowell wasn't sure who was more surprised, himself or Farmer.

Before Lowell could say anything to either Hudson or Farmer, the private had begun turning toward Hudson, wondering just what the hell was going on here.

Farmer was not completely around when a furious Hudson pounded the soldier in the face. Farmer stumbled back, running into Lowell. The sergeant managed to catch his balance and then shoved Farmer forward.

Hudson pasted Farmer another good lick in the face, knocking him down. Cursing the cowardly soldier, Hudson let some of his rage out and began slamming Farmer around.

Lowell and two of the unwounded soldiers—Privates Helmut Hochner and Halsey Butterworth—surged in and tried to pry Hudson away from Farmer. But Hudson was almost maniacal and he easily flung the three men off, clubbing them down when he did. He immediately turned his attentions back to Farmer, beating the soldier unmercifully.

Lowell, Hochner, and Butterworth got up and shook off the effects of Hudson's punches. With a look at each other, they went to wade back into the battle, but Mad Buffalo stepped in front of Lowell.

"Let 'em be," the Cheyenne said easily.

"I can't do that, Mad Buffalo," Lowell protested. "It's not right."

"It's better this way."

Lowell stared into the Indian's eyes a moment, then nodded. "I won't let Linus kill him, though," he insisted.

"If you think that's necessary," Mad Buffalo said with a shrug, "I'll step in when it looks like Farmer's end's near."

Mad Buffalo let it go on for a time, almost enjoying the winces from the other soldiers as every punch landed somewhere on Farmer's body.

At one point, Hudson stepped back to take a short breather. Farmer stood there, more or less, weaving, head down, chest heaving.

"Don't you think he's had enough, Linus?" Lowell called out. He knew he should have done more to stop the beating, but he didn't feel very guilty about not having done so.

"Hell, no," Hudson responded, voice cold and flat.

"And you can tell that dickless maggot sneakin' up behind me there that Mad Buffalo'll stick an arrow up his scrawny ass if he takes more'n another step or two."

Lowell looked over at McKagan. He said nothing, but he didn't have to. The soldier had already started to back off, not wanting to tangle with the fierce-looking Cheyenne. Or with Hudson.

With a smirk, Hudson moved back in on Farmer, pounding him around some more while the others watched. Most of them were stone faced. Even though they were not fond of Farmer, it was hard watching anyone get whaled on the way Farmer was.

Mad Buffalo finally decided that Farmer had had enough. As Hudson took another brief breather, the Cheyenne moved up, grabbed him by the collar of his shirt and yanked him backward a step or two.

"What the hell's wrong with you, boy?" Hudson growled as he jerked himself free of Mad Buffalo's grip.

"He's had enough, Fierce Bear," Mad Buffalo said calmly.

"Like hell he has."

"The bluecoat sergeant don't want you to kill him."

"Like I give a shit what he wants?"

Mad Buffalo shrugged. "Let the blue coats handle it among themselves when we're back at Bent's."

"That don't shine with me, Mad Buffler."

The Cheyenne shrugged. Then he grinned. "Like I give a shit what you want?" he said a little sarcastically.

Reason began returning to Hudson. He finally

smiled a little ruefully. "Goddamn, boy, I hate it when you make sense. Damn savage."

"Just 'cause I'm a damn savage," Mad Buffalo said with a laugh, "don't mean I ain't got more brains than some civilized old shit like you."

"Goddamn arrogant little bastard, too, ain't ya," Hudson asked rhetorically. He sighed. "Ah, well, I suppose ol' shit stick there ain't gonna give us no more trouble for a while." He paused. "We got any food left at all?" he asked, ignoring the bloody mess known as Farmer.

"I got some buffler from yesterday," Mad Buffalo said. "No coffee, though."

"Enough buffler for all of us?"

"If we don't get too greedy."

Hudson nodded and turned. "Stolen Back Woman, get the meat from Mad Buffalo and start cookin' it up."

"I have coffee," Stolen Back Woman said shyly. "In my small pack. And a little pot."

"You do?" Hudson asked, eyes wide.

"A little. Just enough for one cup each, maybe." She seemed embarrassed that she didn't have more. And she was not sure it would be enough to go around, even for one cup each. She decided that she would do without, so that the men could have a full cup each, if need be.

"Well, if that don't beat all. Maybe we ain't as bad off as we figured." He smiled at his wife. "Well, git to makin' it, woman."

"What do we do now?" Lowell asked.

Hudson shrugged. "I got to cogitate on things a

spell. And that ain't a doin' I'd like to handle on an empty stomach." He looked at Lowell. "Whilst we're waitin' for our supper, Sergeant, have your men go see how many of those Mexicans we rubbed out.

They ought to check over the bodies for anything useful, too—food, powder, ball—"

"Private, no!" Lowell suddenly shouted, eyes wide as he looked over Hudson's shoulder.

Farmer had managed to get to his feet and was standing there weaving. His friend McKagan had given him his pistol and Farmer had it in hand. He had gotten it cocked and was trying to bring it to bear on Hudson.

Without seeming to make much effort, Hudson whirled and threw his big butcher knife. The blade sank into Farmer's chest, and Farmer's pistol fired harmlessly into the ground. The soldier hung there a moment, looking dumbly from the horn knife hilt protruding from his chest to Hudson. Then he fell, expiring with a short, whispery gasp.

"As I was sayin'," Hudson continued, as if nothing had happened, "check them bodies for anything we might be able to use. Who knows, maybe one or two of 'em had a knapsack with some food in it."

"Tobacco?" O'Murray asked.

"Hell, you don't bring back some 'baccy, there's somethin' wrong with you, boy," he said more seriously than not.

O'Murray grinned and the soldiers began moving off. Hudson pulled his knife free and wiped it on Farmer's uniform. Then he went to where Stolen Back Woman had gotten a fire going and he sat. The pain in his head was back, and now his hands ached from pounding on Farmer. Waiting for the food, he and Mad Buffalo chatted a little about what to do.

After finishing their meager meal, all the men gathered around Hudson's small fire to assess their situation.

"What'd your boys find on them Mexicans, Sergeant?" Hudson asked when all the men were seated.

"Not a hell of a lot that's useful."

O'Murray grinned and tossed something at Hudson. "Some tobacco for you, Mister Hudson," he said.

"That shines with this ol' hoss," Hudson said, grinning back. "I'm obliged to you, boy."

"No need for that, Mister Hudson. I expect you'll earn that little—and I do mean little—gift before this is all through."

"I reckon I will." There was no doubt in his voice. "So that's all you found, Sergeant? Jist a little 'baccy?"

"Pretty much," Lowell said with a nod. "Some powder and shot, of course, which'll help. And some matches. Other than that, nothing of use. A few pesos here and there. Some personal items that ain't gonna do us much good." He paused, then asked, "So? What do we do?"

"We turn northwest and move as fast as possible. We should be able to cut the Santa Fe Trail in a few days. Maybe we can spot us a wagon train and git us enough supplies to make it to Bent's place."

"Wouldn't it be safer to travel with the wagon train?" Lowell asked.

"Sure, but you ever travel with one of 'em?"

"Well, no," Lowell admitted.

"Slower'n shit, boy. If we find a wagon train up there soon off and get some horses, we can git to Bent's in another couple days. Travelin' with them goddamn wagons'll take us a week. Maybe more. Besides, I ain't particular about which way the train's goin' if we can get some horses and supplies." Lowell nodded. "Yes, it could be headed east, couldn't it?"

"Yep."

"So we're givin' up?" Lowell asked after a few moments.

"Fuck no," Hudson said vehemently. "We get to Bent's, we can get some more horses and supplies."

"Mister Bent was rather low on both, last I heard."

"We'll find enough. Don't you worry about that."

"It might take us out of the fight," Lowell said edgily. He had come too far now to be pulled off this mission.

"If the army keeps anywhere close to the schedule Kearny figured on, they're not there, which means they can't say anything to you. If they are still there, yeah, they might pull you off this venture. On the other hand, they might not. Kearny finds out how much trouble we've had, what with the Comanches and the Mexicans, he jist might send us back out— with a heap of reinforcements."

"I don't know how likely that is," Lowell said doubtfully.

"Might not be likely at all. But Kearny ain't gonna be fond of what's happened to his men and I reckon he'll want some punishment handed out."

Lowell still looked skeptical.

"Another thing to consider, is that if they ain't there, we can go back out again. And this time we might maybe get us some help from Mad Buffler's people. Might be some other of the old mountaineers up at the post, too. Those boys always take to a good fight. I aim to kick some Mexican ass now—after we do so with the Comanches."

"It's gonna be kind of late for our men by then, ain't it?" Lowell asked sadly. "The captives, I mean."

"Good chance of it." Then he shrugged. "But that don't make no difference now."

"What?" Lowell erupted, surprised. "You don't think it's important that those men're gonna be traded off to the Mexicans?"

"That ain't likely to happen," Hudson said flatly. He was tired of all this. He simply wanted to kill some Comanches—and some Mexican soldiers—now and be done with it.

"But you said ... ?"

"I know what the fuck I said," Hudson snapped. His patience and what little joviality he might have had were long gone. "I was givin' you a line of shit to keep you and your boys goin'. I was plannin' all the time to find me some goddamn Comanches to rub out for them havin' put Whirlin' Storm under. Now I aim to add Mexican soldiers to the pot."

"Goddamn you, Hudson," Lowell snapped. He was furious at having been duped.

Hudson was unfazed by Lowell's fury.

"Why the goddamn hell didn't you just tell me that? Christ, I thought you knew me well enough by then to know that I ain't the kind that gives up too easy. I was ready to turn back then out of frustration and annoyance. But goddammit, to convince me to go on, all you had to do was tell me you wanted to avenge Whirling Storm's death. Hell, that would've been enough."

Hudson shrugged. "I didn't know that at the time. I ain't so sure now that it would've worked then. You got your own mission to worry about—gettin' those blue coats back. I had my own reasons for pushin' on then. And," he added harshly, "I got even more reason for keepin' goin' now, goddammit. I ain't about to let no fuckin' soldados run off all my stock and plunder and git away with it."

"I thought you liked Mexicans," Lowell said, trying to contain his anger. What was done was done and could not be changed. He had to think about what happened now.

"I generally do," Hudson said with a shrug. "Less'n they try'n kill me. Same thing with Injins. I ain't got no dislikin' for the Comanches in general. 'Course I ain't got much likin' for 'em either. But I don't hate 'em jist for bein' Comanches. Same with the Mexicans. Or the Americans, for that matter. There's a heap of folks I can't abide—not because they're Americans or Mexicans or Comanches or Utes but because they're assholes as people."

"Very noble," Lowell said a little sarcastically. He was still hot about being duped by Hudson, and while he was succeeding fairly well in keeping his temper in check, he could not resist getting in a shot when he could.

"Ain't a goddamn thing noble about it, boy," Hudson said evenly. He knew Lowell was angry. He also knew Lowell couldn't do anything about it. "It jist makes sense is all. Hell, a man can come up with more'n enough enemies jist by makin' his way through life. Why the hell should I go out of my way to make heaps more without good reason? No, sir, I'll take my enemies one man at a time, more or less, rather than makin' 'em wholesale."

Lowell was beginning to dislike it when Hudson was reasonable. Especially when it served to undercut his anger at the former mountain man. "Well, goddammit," he said lamely, "if you ever got somethin' to complain about with me, just tell me. If I resist then, well we'll have to work it out."

"I don't expect I'll have to go pullin' your leg no more." Lowell nodded, anger mostly dissipated now. Anger would do him no good here. The decision had been made, now they all had to try to make it work. "What about food and such?" he asked.

"Water's our biggest problem. We got enough here that would last us long enough to get back to Bent's—if we had any way of carryin' it. But we got no canteens."

"We got one," Butterworth said. "I found one near a Mexican's body. It must have fallen off his saddle."

Hudson nodded. "That won't take us far, but we should be able to find some water now and again," he said. "We have enough powder and shot for huntin', and we should be able to jump a buffler or some deer or something. We'll make it," he added with more confidence in his voice than he felt.

"We leave in the mornin'?" Lowell asked.

Hudson thought it over a minute. "Nope," he finally answered, shaking his head gently. "Mornin' after, as early as we can. The boys've been in a hell of a fight today, and we got a couple of wounded. A day's rest'll help us all recover some, and we can make better time. Besides, we've been a mite parched the last few days, and with more of such facin' us, it might be a good idea to git as much water in us as we can hold."

Hudson looked from one man to the other. He was generally pleased with what he saw. McKagan might give them a little trouble, but Hudson doubted it. Even the foul-looking Elroy Hogg seemed to be determined.

CHAPTER 16

After the little gathering broke up, Lowell lingered a bit. "I don't much like the idea, but I'd as soon leave those dead soldiers out there as bury 'em," he said quietly, ashamed that he would suggest such a thing.

"No skin off my ass," Hudson responded easily. "Far's I'm concerned, they don't deserve any burial at all, let alone a decent one."

Lowell was relieved but still feeling guilty. "I sort of hoped you'd agree with me. Not so much that they don't deserve to be buried but because of the work it'd take my men. They're already bushed from all the travelin', plus a couple are wounded and all."

"Ain't no reason to put your men through all that, as far as I can see, Sergeant."

Lowell nodded. "Good. Then I'll just have the men bury Private Farmer."

"He don't deserve a decent burial either, by my lights," Hudson said flatly.

"I can't leave him out there for the wolves and buzzards," Lowell said, only a little shocked.

"Like hell you can't. That shit stick was nothin' but trouble right from the start. And if it wasn't for him, we might not be in this predicament. You ask me, I'd let the scavengers have him."

"I'll take that under consideration," Lowell said, standing. He turned and left, pondering the situation. He didn't care much whether Farmer was buried or not, but he figured it was almost a requirement that he do so. As bad as Farmer was, he was still a fellow soldier. That ought to be worth something, Lowell figured.

The group was in considerably better health after a day of little work and lots of rest. Mad Buffalo shot two deer early in the day and then a small buffalo cow later. They ate well and often throughout the day. In between filling their stomachs, they hurriedly jerked a fair portion of the meat.

They finally pulled out just after dawn the following day and plodded northwest. As Hudson led his small group across one of the creeks, he saw Farmer's body still lying out in the open. It had been hauled away from their camp a little and scavengers of various kinds had worked busily on the corpse for most of the day before. What was left of Farmer was not a pretty sight. Few of the men paid the squalid thing much attention.

The heat was still staggering, hovering around 100 degrees that day and for the next two, as it had been every day since the rainstorm. The nights were cold and traveling through the harsh land wore on them steadily.

They found no water that first day nor the second,

but early on the third they came across a creek with a few muddy puddles of water. The men and woman slurped greedily at the dirty water. With a little bit of relief, they moved on an hour later.

That night, they stayed along another creek. There was no water to be seen, but with a little digging, they managed to raise some water up through the sandy creek bottom. Mad Buffalo had also taken a buffalo that day and so they had fresh meat to go with the lifegiving water.

The maddeningly brutal sun the next day, though, quashed their lightly uplifted spirits fairly swiftly and they stumbled along disheartened, except for Hudson, Mad Buffalo, and Stolen Back Woman. Lowell didn't feel too sorry for himself, but he felt bad for his men, and that served to keep his humor in check.

But that afternoon, Mad Buffalo trotted back to the column. Hudson had offered him the opportunity to stay with everyone else since they were all on foot now, but the Cheyenne had opted to continue his scouting duties and so for the five days since the fight with the Mexican soldiers, Mad Buffalo had usually ranged well out ahead of the small group.

Now he stopped in front of Hudson.

"Somethin' wrong?" Lowell asked, moving up to stand alongside Hudson.

"Village," Mad Buffalo said.

"Comanche?"

"Out here it can't be nothin' else," Hudson answered. He looked at Mad Buffalo. "How far?"

"Three, four miles."

Hudson nodded. That was about right, he figured. They were about as close to the village as he wanted to get right now. At this distance, there was little chance the Comanches would spot them. That would allow them to do what needed doing.

"How're we going to get around it?" Lowell sighed at this latest difficulty to overcome.

"We ain't goin' around it," Hudson said, looking at Lowell as if the man had lost his reason. Once he thought about it, Hudson decided it was possible that Lowell had. Or any of them had. Maybe all of them. It wouldn't be such a strange thing in a land like this, not with what they all had encountered.

Lowell was surprised but managed to hide most of it. "You think our missin' men are there?" he asked dumbly.

Hudson shrugged. "I don't give a shit whether your damned friends're there or not. Them Comanches've got horses, though."

It was Lowell's turn to look at Hudson like he had gone mad. "You can't be serious," he said, doubt thick in his voice.

"You want to wager on that, boy?" Hudson countered, voice suddenly gone harsh.

"I ain't got anything to wager, even if I wanted to," Lowell said stiffly.

"Like hell you don't."

"What can I bet?" Lowell asked, befuddled.

"Your life," Hudson answered flatly. "And you might not have a chance to decide whether to make the wager. We don't get some goddamn horses soon, we might not make it back to Bent's."

"I thought you said we'd cut the Santa Fe Trail by now," Lowell said testily.

"We're gittin' close," Hudson said, not liking to have to admit he had been wrong in his calculations, though it wasn't all his fault. "But it could still be a couple more days at the rate we're goin'."

"You sayin' my men're slowin' us down too much?" Lowell asked defensively.

"We're all slowin' us down too much," Hudson said, trying to soothe the sergeant a little. "Was it maybe jist me'n Mad Buffler here, we could've made better time, I suppose, but my head's still painin' me some, and that don't help matters none."

Lowell nodded, angry at himself for having gotten angry at Hudson.

"Maybe we shoulda gone due north," Mad Buffalo said into the breach, almost as if musing.

"Might've been better," Hudson agreed. "But it's too late for that now. Even if we turned straight north, we'd still have at least another day, maybe two or three, of walking."

"So we just up and walk into that camp?" Lowell asked. He was angry enough at everyone and everything, but mostly himself and their situation, to be ready to try anything, including a frontal assault on a Comanche village.

"That'd get us all put under for certain, boy. We'll wait till dark. Then jist me'n Mad Buffler'll slip in there and do what's needed."

"What if you don't come back?"

Hudson shrugged. "Then you and your boys'll be on your own, Sergeant." He almost laughed. "Say a prayer for us, if you're of a mind to, and then be on your way agin. Jist try'n see that Stolen Back Woman gits back to her village. Or to Bent's. Bill'll see that she gits home."

"That's heartening," Lowell said dryly. He almost managed a smile. "So, we camp right where we are?"

"Not camp, no. Jist set here and wait. No fires. We can eat jerky, rest up a little. We'll move as soon as dark falls. Me'n Mad Buffalo'll leave you and the rest—includin' Stolen Back Woman—about a mile from the village. When we git back ..."

"If you get back," Lowell corrected.

"When we git back, we'll head out right off. I want to be as far away from this goddamn village as we can be by mornin'. So, since it looks like we're facin' a long night, Sergeant, I suggest you have your men try'n get some sleep for the afternoon."

"I'll order it," Lowell said with a shake of his head. "But in this heat and with no cover—plus knowin' there's a village of Comanches right over yonder, I doubt many of the men're gonna get much rest."

Hudson shrugged. He could do nothing about that. He would sleep as well as he could. So would Mad Buffalo. Both men, having lived most or all of their lives in the wilderness, had learned to partake of rest, food, and water whenever opportunity arose. "Well, if they gotta be up, have at least one of 'em keep watch facin' north. Have another watch the other three directions, walkin' in an arc."

"Why?" Lowell asked. "At least why the second man? The village is northwest. Any Comanches come, it'll be from that way, won't it?"

"You never heard of a Comanche huntin' party? Or a war party? Or another band comin' to visit their friends and relatives?"

"Oh," Lowell offered, feeling like an idiot.

Soon after, Hudson and his wife stepped off a few paces from the rest of the men. Stolen Back Woman lay down on her back, using a blanket—one of the few things she had had in a pouch she had taken off her horse just before the battle—as a pillow under her head. Hudson lay at right angles to her and rested his head on her stomach. He pulled his hat down over his eyes and was asleep in minutes.

Stolen Back Woman woke her husband as the sun was going down. Hudson sat up and rubbed his face. He stood and walked over to where Lowell was. He was a little surprised to see that the sergeant was asleep. He went off to visit O'Murray, who was guarding the north side. "See anything, Private?" he asked.

"Not a blessed goddamn thing, sir. A couple of hawks or somethin' earlier, but other'n that, I got the impression we're the only livin' things God's left down here on earth. I ain't ever seen a place so desolate as this." He almost shuddered. His Irish soul craved companionship—the more people the merrier, as far as he was concerned—and being in such a place as this was almost too much for him to bear.

"Is right lonely, ain't it?" Hudson said. He thought it just fine. He was not one who enjoyed the company of large numbers of people. One of the things that had attracted him to the mountains in the first place was the solitude. It took him a little getting used to it, but he had come to prefer that kind of life. With the exception of wanting Stolen Back Woman and maybe a few close friends, like Mad Buffalo, around, he was content to be by himself. Cities, even ones as small as Taos, drove him to distraction after only a short time.

"It's damn near unholy, sir," O'Murray said.

Hudson grinned a little. "You jist hold on, Private. We'll git you back to civilization yet."

O'Murray laughed. "I don't mean to complain, sir. It's just that such a place leaves this Irish boy's soul reelin' with superstition."

Hudson patted O'Murray on the shoulder. He knew the Irishman would not wilt under the face of adversity, whether real or imagined. He was just garrulous and wanted to talk such strange things out a little. Hudson himself had been more than a little impressed the first time he found himself in a place like this. It was awesome, and fear inspiring, if one let his imagination run away with him.

He went back and sat beside Stolen Back Woman. He ate some buffalo jerky and took a few sips of water they had in the canteen. There was little left. Mad Buffalo joined them a few minutes later and they ate in silence. There was no need for the former mountain man and the Cheyenne to discuss what they would do soon.

Done eating, Hudson went over to Lowell and lightly kicked the bottom of the soldier's boot.

Lowell woke slowly and groggily. His face was shiny with sweat, and his uniform damp. "Jesus

Christ, this heat's unbearable," he grumbled. He pushed himself wearily to his feet. "It time, Linus?" he asked.

"Jist about. Have your men eat some jerky. The canteen's about half full. You and the men can finish it off. Soon's you're all done, we'll head out."

Lowell nodded and moved off, calling out orders. Hudson turned and headed north a little way. Standing there with his rifle cradled in his left arm, he kept watch while the soldiers ate. Mad Buffalo did the same duty around the rest of the camp.

It was not quite full dark when the small group began moving once again. The people stayed pretty close together, except for Mad Buffalo, who went ahead to keep watch. The Cheyenne was waiting for the others about half a mile from the Comanche village.

"Lay on this ridge here," he said to Lowell, "and you can keep an eye on things without bein' seen." He pointed to where they could see some fires glowing dimly in the dark.

"It's too goddamn dark to see anything," Lowell grumbled. The walk had made him sweat again, but now that he had stopped, the night's cool temperatures and the wind chilled him. It, along with everything else these days, irritated him.

"The moon and stars'll be out in full soon," Hudson said. He, too, was irritated. He should've never gotten involved with all this. If he hadn't, Whirling Storm would still be alive and he would be having himself a fine spree in the Cheyenne village. With the United States at war with Mexico, a spree in Taos or Santa Fe would've been out of the question in any case. "You'll be able to see some then. You keep an eye on the horizon, you should be able to see anyone comin' out of that village."

"Sure we will," Lowell said skeptically. Then he grinned wearily. "Ah, hell, Linus, I'm just bein' an old worrywart."

Hudson nodded, understanding. "You and the boys jist set here and relax, if you can," he said. "Me'n Mad Buffler'll be back soon's we can. And, for chrissakes, don't go shootin' us by mistake."

"We'll try," Lowell said dryly. More seriously, he added, "Good luck, Linus. Or should I say good medicine?"

"Either way shines."

"Then I hope you have good medicine. You and Mad Buffalo both."

Hudson nodded.

"God go with you, Mister Hudson," O'Murray said quietly. "And with you, too, Mad Buffalo," he added, "if such a thing don't offend."

Mad Buffalo smiled a little. "I'll take all the help I can get, blue coat. Includin' your God's."

Hudson and Mad Buffalo made their plans, such as they were. There was not much planning they could do, really. They just needed to know what each other would be doing at any moment.

Hudson checked his Colts, making sure all five chambers were loaded. He also made sure he had extra powder, shot, and caps in his belt pouch. He handed his rifle to Stolen Back Woman. "Goddamn thing'll jist git in my way," he said. Then he looked at Mad Buffalo. The Cheyenne nodded at him and the two men headed out, trotting at a good pace.

When they were a hundred yards or so from the first lodges, they stopped to get their breath back. Then they split up, Hudson going westward, Mad Buffalo eastward.

CHAPTER 17

Hudson did not worry about the pack of half-wild dogs that was in every Comanche camp, as it was in every other Indian village he knew of. The animals generally barked and snarled so much that the Comanches most likely wouldn't notice anything out of the ordinary when Hudson and Mad Buffalo entered the camp.

As he expected, the dogs picked up his scent moments after he began edging past lodges. In a few more seconds, he was surrounded by a yapping pack of mongrels. Most backed off when he darted a hand toward them or something, but one big, dingy great cur was persistent in annoying him. It became so much trouble that an irritated Hudson finally stopped.

Waiting a moment, he slid out his tomahawk, then brained the offending animal. The dog yelped once before dying, but Hudson figured no one would be alarmed by that either. He was at least moderately grateful that the other dogs stayed behind to sniff the still quivering carcass as he moved on. Before he had gotten twenty feet more, he heard the dogs growling at each other as they fought over their companion's remains.

"That ought to keep you shit sticks occupied for a spell," Hudson muttered as he pushed on.

He stopped behind a lodge and listened intently. He heard some snores, but no voices. Creeping around the side, he eased into the tipi through the flap and moved immediately to the side a few feet. He crouched, letting his eyes adjust a little. Then he crept around the lodge, picking up two parfleches of jerky, and three buffalo bladders used as canteens. They were full of water.

Slipping back outside, he hurried to where he and Mad Buffalo had split up and dropped his stolen supplies. Then he hurried back into the village. He froze, squatting in the shadows of a lodge when he saw a Comanche family—a man, two women, and two children—stop at the lodge and call for entrance. When they had gone inside, he moved on, thinking he knew which tipi that family had just left to go visiting.

Hudson sliced open the rear of that lodge and eased himself inside. With no one in there, he could move about more freely. He found a coffeepot on the fire. With a small smile, he dumped the contents on one of the buffalo sleeping robes. He stuffed the coffeepot into a buckskin sack. Within two minutes, he had added a substantial amount of coffee, a little sugar he found, and some salt. He found three more full water containers—two large gourds and another buffalo bladder.

Arms laden, he went back out the way he had come in and brought his plunder out of the village and put it with the rest. Once more he headed back into the village.

Hudson found another lodge that was unoccupied for now, and he went in through a slit he cut in the side. He had collected some berries, roots, a haunch of smoked deer, coffee, sugar, and water and was about to leave when he heard someone at the flap.

"Shit," he thought. He dropped to one knee and set down his stolen property. By the time a young woman stepped inside, Hudson had moved around the circular tipi several feet away from the things he had set down and stood, trying not to breathe too much.

The Comanche stopped, as if suspecting something wasn't right. She peered around but saw nothing out of the ordinary. She finally shrugged and walked toward the back of the tipi—and where Hudson had put his loot. She shrugged out of her dress and dropped it.

Hudson almost sucked in a breath. In the dim firelight, the young woman presented a delicious picture. She had nicely formed legs, and her back was smooth and supple looking. Her buttocks were a little plump, but Hudson had no problem with that. The thought of a roll in the robes with this young woman was intriguing to Hudson, though he knew it was simply a fantasy and a ridiculous one at that.

The woman bent to remove her leggings, giving Hudson another interesting view of her. Then she went to sit on the robe—and her naked buttocks encountered Hudson's pile of plunder. She jumped up, gasping, and spun. She knelt, fingers lifting some of the items that had materialized right where she was going to sit.

Hudson stepped forward, sliding out his tomahawk. He moved swiftly, but silently. The woman was still kneeling, wondering what had happened here, when Hudson smacked her on the temple with the flat side of the weapon. He didn't really want to kill her, though he would feel no guilt if it happened. She might be a beautiful and enticing young woman, but she was a Comanche—at this point an enemy.

He grabbed the woman by the hair and dragged her off the pile of booty. He grabbed the goods and then moved out, fast. When he got back to where the rest of the stolen property was, Mad Buffalo was there with a dozen Comanche ponies. Hudson put the latest load down. "How'd it go?" he asked.

"No trouble," Mad Buffalo replied. "You?"

"Had to club down a woman who came into the last lodge I was in." There was no need to explain that he could not have afforded to allow her to see him and raise an alarm.

"You put her under?"

Hudson shrugged. "Ain't sure. I walloped her a pretty good shot with the side of my 'hawk, but I didn't split her head open."

"We better go then."

"We need another load or two of supplies."

"No," Mad Buffalo said firmly. "We got enough." He switched to speaking Cheyenne. "If that woman's dead, she might be found any time. We leave here now, we could be miles away before that happens. If she's not dead, she might wake soon and spread the alarm. Either way, we'll have Comanches on our trail before we get far."

"I told you before I didn't like it when you made sense," Hudson responded in Cheyenne. "All right, you keep an eye on the horses to make sure they don't go anywhere. I'll load these supplies."

Mad Buffalo nodded. He moved among the small knot of horses. "What did you get?" he asked softly.

"Coffee, jerky, a little fresh deer, sugar, a little salt, and a number of canteens," Hudson answered as he hung bags and boxes over horses' backs with lengths of rope cut from a coil he had taken from the village.

"Canteens full?"

"Nope," Hudson said sarcastically. "I poked around until I found empty ones." He went back to his work. It didn't take long to finish since there wasn't all that much.

Then he and Mad Buffalo each mounted a pony and rode off. They went slowly at first, not wanting to create any ruckus that might alert the village. A mile away, though, they broke into a gallop, herding the other horses ahead of them. Less than two hours after they had left, Hudson and Mad Buffalo were back with their traveling companions.

"Goddamn, if you didn't do it," Lowell said in wonder as the two men brought the horses to a stop.

"Told you we would. Maybe you'll start to believe me when I tell you somethin'," Hudson said as he dismounted.

"Ain't likely after that whopper you handed me about the Comanches ransomin' our men," Lowell said only a little bit testily. He had almost gotten over it.

"Everything I said then could happen, boy," Hudson said easily. "It ain't likely, maybe, but they could do what I said. And if they did, it'd be for the reasons I said, and they'd do it the way I said."

"Hell, Linus, I'm pretty sure you're right about that. Not that it matters now. I just wanted to get in a shot at you—kind of to let you know I ain't forgotten it but I've given up worryin' over it."

A smile twitched at Hudson's lips. "I'm relieved," he said dryly. "Now, Sergeant, git your men mounted and let's make some tracks. I hope your men can handle ridin' bareback."

"Speakin' for myself—and, I think, the rest of the men—if it'd get us out of here and away from those Comanches, I'd carry the horse."

Hudson nodded and helped Stolen Back Woman up onto a pony. He took his rifle in hand and then jumped on another horse. "Now, let's go find us some missin' blue coats," Hudson said grimly.

They moved off at a good pace, but one that would not hurt the animals. In the dark, they traveled close together, not wanting anyone to get lost. Hudson, Mad Buffalo and Lowell rode abreast at the head of the group, leading them mostly in a southerly direction. Stolen Back Woman rode directly behind her man. The extra horses came next, driven by the soldiers, who rode in a loose arc behind the ponies.

Hudson kept the group going throughout the

night and about an hour before dawn, he and Mad Buffalo found a wash that had some water at the bottom, two stunted trees, and some brush. They called a halt, deciding to camp there.

While some of the men tended the horses, others found fuel and then built fires. Before long, coffee was heating and the piece of deer meat was cooking, as well as some antelope Mad Buffalo had taken just before they stopped. While they waited, the men did whatever other chores were needed. There weren't many, but there was enough work to keep them all busy for at least a bit as they waited for their meal.

When the men got to eating, it was almost like a party for them. They gorged on antelope and slurped down hot coffee thickened with plenty of sugar. The feast, which it was for them after their latest five-day trek, made their spirits rise as high as the smoke from their fires.

They spent that day there and the night, too. They filled up ort food and coffee. The following morning, rested and well fed, they rode off, turning more southwesterly. For Hudson, it was the best way to head. With horses, some supplies and enough water to last them for at least a little while, they felt almost on top of the world.

The men seemed to have become tougher, stronger, more determined overnight. Once Hudson and Mad Buffalo had come back from that Comanche village with the horses and supplies, the soldiers had become a different group. Because of that, they were willing, almost eager, to spend long hours on the back of a horse, and do so without much complaint.

Still, when they left that little camp, they were a hardened, angry group of men. All of them had visions of avenging their fellow soldiers' captivity, and possibly death, against the Comanches. And all wanted revenge for their defeat at the hands of the Mexican soldiers. Even McKagan, who was still bitter at Hudson for killing Farmer, was one of the men now in his desire to fulfill what had become a duty.

Over the next couple of days, they moved fast and steadily, stopping only occasionally during the day to rest the horses a little. It also gave the men time to ease their aching rumps. Only Mad Buffalo was used to riding without a saddle. They made camp wherever they were when darkness fell; filled their canteens whenever they found water; hunted as the need and opportunity arose. Mad Buffalo had little trouble keeping them in fresh meat.

The Cheyenne took up his usual position ahead of the group, always searching for sign of the Comanches. Though he had not made any statement about it to the soldiers, Hudson had told the Cheyenne to also watch for sign of the Mexicans who had attacked them. Hudson was fairly certain they would never find them, but he didn't want to miss an opportunity for retribution for lack of attentiveness.

Mad Buffalo found no sign of the Mexicans, but sometime during the afternoon of the second day after stealing the horses, Mad Buffalo reported that he had spotted a Comanche village a few miles ahead.

Hudson had the soldiers stop and wait. Then he and Mad Buffalo rode out, heading for the village. Hudson dismounted at a low ridge. As Mad Buffalo rode toward the village, Hudson clambered to the top of the knoll and lay along the top to watch.

Mad Buffalo didn't return until past dark. Once he was back with Hudson, he shook his head. "The blue coats ain't there," he said in English.

"You sure?"

"Yes."

"Were they ever there?"

"Don't think so. I think someone would've said somethin' about it while I was visitin'. Especially if they'd been killed there."

He nodded. "What'd you tell 'em when you rode in?"

"Just said I was lookin' to steal ponies from the Mexicans—or the Texans. Said that since the People and the Comanches're friends now, I saw their village and thought I'd stop."

Hudson nodded again. It all sounded plausible enough. "What took you so long to git back?"

"Worried about me?" Mad Buffalo asked with a laugh.

"In a pig's ass. I jist thought maybe you was kissin' ass with those goddamn Comanches down there.

"That's me. Mad Buffalo, the Comanche lover. I had to enjoy their hospitality," Mad Buffalo added a little sarcastically. "I didn't want them to get suspicious."

"Good thing. You tell 'em you were leavin'?"

"Nope. That's why I waited till after dark. I

figured it'd be better if I just pretended I was gonna stay the night with them and then rode out when dark came."

Hudson nodded again. "Well, we best git back to the others, lest they fret themselves into a frenzy."

The same basic scenario played itself out again twice more in the next three days, as they found other Comanche villages. Those occasions produced no more success than the first, and frustration began to settle over the group again.

A week after stealing the ponies from the Comanches, though, Mad Buffalo returned to the column during the late morning.

"Another village?" Hudson asked. He did not look forward to another disappointment.

"Nope," Mad Buffalo said in English. He grinned grimly. "I found the Mexican long knives, though. They're holed up in a little canyon on the Canadian. About five miles southwest."

"You boys mind rubbin' out some goddamn Mexican soldados first, before we raise hair on some Comanches?" Hudson asked in general, looking from soldier to soldier. When he received no dissent, he said harshly, "Then let's go pay those shit sticks a visit."

CHAPTER 18

They rode into the small canyon from the east. It was an easy ride since the canyon didn't really appear to go down; it was more that the surrounding land seemed to rise. On the south side, the plains were not too much higher than where they rode, gradually rising and then flattening. The north side, however, suddenly shot up in a steep cliff of a hundred feet or so. The canyon tapered back into nothingness only a half mile or so west of where the group entered it.

There was water in the river, though it did not completely cover the width of the wide riverbed, and it was shallow. Few trees were to be found, but there were some stunted ones. And the brush was fairly copious. It was, all in all, Hudson decided, a decent place to spend a few days and partake of stolen plunder. The decision did not, however, alter his hatred of the Mexican soldiers.

Suddenly Hudson jerked his horse to a halt. The others followed suit, wondering what was wrong. "Jesus, I've been a goddamn fool," he muttered as

Mad Buffalo and Lowell eased up alongside him.

"What about?" Lowell asked.

Hudson pointed to the top of the cliff that towered over the canyon not far ahead on their right.

"Someone up there?" Lowell asked, squinting, trying to see.

"I don't goddamn know," Hudson hissed, anger at himself boiling rapidly in him now. "That's the goddamn problem."

Mad Buffalo nodded. "I should've thunk of it, too." He turned his pony. "I'll be back soon," he said before racing off back thy way they had come, past a knot of startled, befuddled soldiers.

"Don't be so hard on yourself, Linus," Lowell said evenly.

"People who make stupid goddamn mistakes like this don't last long out here, Sergeant," Hudson said sourly. "I ain't made it out here all these years by bein' a thoughtless fool. Shit." He paused. "I should've thought right off when I saw this place that if they had any guards out, they'd certainly have one sittin' up there watchin' things. It might be too late already."

"Maybe it won't be so bad," Lowell said lamely.

Hudson didn't answer; didn't even look at the sergeant. He simply sat on his horse and filled and lit his pipe. Lowell kept his silence, too.

It was almost an hour before Mad Buffalo returned and Hudson was in a high dander by then. He said nothing about the time, though.

"No one's there," Mad Buffalo announced.

"You sure?" Hudson asked, surprised.

"Goddamn, yes, I'm sure," Mad Buffalo retorted.

"Either those greasers packed up and left already or they're the dumbest bastards I've ever come across."

"I think they're jist stupid bastards," Mad Buffalo opined.

"Let's hope so." Most of his anger having fled, Hudson led the way along the river, going slow because the mud clutched at the ponies' hooves. Before long they spotted the Mexican camp and they eased to a halt.

"Don't look like they're very alert," Lowell said warily.

"I'll be damned," Hudson muttered. He could not believe the Mexican soldiers had no guards out. Indeed, it looked as if the entire camp was asleep. He was glad, though, that the soldados were not being vigilant. It would make the grisly job facing his group so much easier.

"They couldn't have been expecting us," Lowell said. He almost winced when Mad Buffalo gave him a look of scorn and he wondered why.

"That's a fact, boy," Hudson said. "But out here, if you ain't keepin' watch for the Comanches, you're gonna wind up rubbed out for certain."

"Oh," Lowell responded, feeling like an utter idiot.

Hudson considered rubbing it in a little more, but he didn't have the heart for it right now. He was too focused on what had to be done here. "Have someone stay here with Stolen Back Woman to watch the horses," he said, dismounting. "Pick whoever you want, but make sure he's trustworthy." He didn't need to name McKagan.

"Gonna be a hard choice," Lowell said proudly. "There ain't a one of my boys gonna want to stay out of this fight." He, too, dismounted, rubbing his seat. This riding bareback was not easy for him.

"That's a good sign," Hudson acknowledged. "But it's got to be. I ain't aimin' to lose those goddamn ponies again."

"What happens if we get our own animals back?" Lowell asked, interested.

"I aim to ride my horse. Goddamn thing's been a good animal and I'm comfortable on him. You and the rest can do what you want."

"What'll we do with these stolen Comanche horses then?"

"Sell 'em to Bill Bent when we git back to the fort. The goddamn army owes me that much,"

"The army ain't about to let me and the boys get any gain from it," Lowell said with a combination of wistfulness and sourness.

Hudson grinned just a bit. "That's a fact. But ain't no army can tell me I cain't spend my newfound wealth with some friends, now is there?"

Lowell smiled. "That's a fact," he responded. He walked back to his men, towing his, Hudson's, and Mad Buffalo's ponies behind him. He talked with his soldiers a few moments. Then Stolen Back Woman and a downcast Private Sean O'Murray moved off a ways with all the horses. Lowell and the four other soldiers walked back up to where Hudson and Mad Buffalo stood, looking out at the Mexican camp.

"What's the plan of action?" Lowell asked, almost

officiously.

"What fuckin' plan?" Hudson snorted. "I aim to walk in there and rub out as many of those shit sticks as I can as fast as I can. I suggest you and your boys do the same."

Hudson nodded. He had no problem with the cold heartedness of it. These particular Mexican soldiers deserved whatever they got, as far as he was concerned. While not fond of killing at all, let alone wholesale slaughter, Sergeant Alfred Lowell was a man who took his duty seriously, and he would not shirk from it no matter how bad it was. He thought his men felt about the same, but he thought he better check. "Any of you men have a problem with that?" he asked, looking from one soldier to the next.

Each shook his head. There was determination in their eyes, as well as a desire for revenge.

"You certain, boys?" Lowell pressed.

"Ve're Americans, by Gott, und damn proud of it," Private Helmut Hochner said with a touch of arrogance. "Ve're not—or at least I'm not—about to let a bunch of gottdamn foul Mexican soldiers vhip our asses und get avay vit' it. Those men haff much punishment comink, and I plan to be among those handink it out."

"I agree with Helmut, Sergeant," Private Halsey Butterworth tacked on.

"Me, too, goddammit," Private Elroy Hogg said. The slimy-looking soldier spit tobacco juice. "I'll be dead and buried hunnert years befo' I let some goddamn greasers git away with sich shit and you can wager on that."

Even McKagan nodded, his face set in determination.

Lowell nodded and looked at Hudson. "Ready when you are, Mister Hudson."

The former mountain man did not see that a reply was needed. He simply turned and began walking slowly toward the camp. "You want to git the horses? Or you want to rub out Mexicans?" Hudson asked, looking at his Cheyenne friend.

"Get the ponies." Mad Buffalo grinned viciously. "I can kill Mexicans any time."

"Chickenshit," Hudson teased.

"That's me," Mad Buffalo responded without batting an eye.

Lowell shook his head, wondering how the two could banter at such a time. He was as nervous as a cat. Not afraid, just concerned that something would go wrong and that he would lose some of his men.

As he walked, Hudson pulled out his two Colts, and swiftly loaded the fifth chamber of each. He had the feeling he would need every shot he could get. His rifle was slung across his back, a hunk of horsehair rope made into a temporary sling. It would be out of his way there, but yet accessible in a hurry if he needed it. But for close in work, which this would be, for the most part, he preferred the .36-caliber revolvers.

As they neared the loosely made camp, the men began moving away from each other some, spreading out to make a wide sweep through the camp. Mad Buffalo, silent as a ghost's shadow, headed toward the herd of horses. The animals were feeding on the skimpy grass and drinking water on a little patch of land that jutted up out of the river.

One Mexican had gotten up and was facing away from Hudson's group, urinating on a small sagebrush. Hudson shot him in the back. The man emitted a surprised gasp and then fell forward, landing on the sagebrush.

The shot did little to rouse the camp but the fusillade from the soldiers had more effect. Soldados began scrambling up, reaching for rifles, pistols, or swords. They seemed confused, disoriented. Hudson realized as he shot another one at pointblank range that most if not all of them were drunk. Where they had gotten that much whiskey was a mystery to Hudson.

Soldados began running when they realized their camp had been invaded. Most did not bother to learn that their attackers were well outnumbered. They figured they were under siege by a superior force and they reacted accordingly. Some fled across the shallow river and up the sometimes steeply carved banks, trying to get to the prairie beyond.

Others tried to get to the horses and were given a rude surprise when they found themselves being shot down with arrows from a howling, painted face Cheyenne who seemed to have risen from the depths of hell.

Still more of the survivors of the initial attack raced on foot up the canyon, toward the west, to where it tapered off and leveled out onto the plains. Hogg and Butterworth went chasing after them, stopping just long enough to fire their single-shot rifles once each.

Lowell ran toward the herd, figuring to help Mad Buffalo, though the Cheyenne did not really seem to need any aid. He shot down one soldado who appeared to be trying to get around Mad Buffalo's little island and attack the Cheyenne from the rear. Then he was at Mad Buffalo's side, calming horses and mules while the Indian fended off the swiftly diminishing attacks from the Mexicans.

Hudson and Hochner moved through the camp, the soldier wielding a sword he had grabbed from a soldado he had shot.

Hudson fired his revolvers smoothly and with frightening efficiency, at least until the camp was deserted, which took only moments. Finally, he stopped and reloaded his pistols, filling only four chambers in each this time. He did not think the fifth chambers would be needed. Then he spotted the lieutenant that had led the group of soldados.

The officer had gone downriver a little ways and then crossed the water. The bank there was more gradual and lower, so he had a much easier time of making it to the plains. As the lieutenant disappeared over the canyon rim, Hudson charged toward the horses, shoving his pistols away as he ran. His rifle slapped against his back and buttocks.

Hudson saw his own horse in the midst of the herd. He shoved his way through the milling animals until he got to his own mount. He patted the horse's neck a few moments, speaking softly. The horse recognized him and nuzzled his cheek. Hudson jumped on the animal's back. Grabbing a handful of mane, he pulled it around. The horse responded with a few eager hops and jumps, seemingly glad to have his master riding him again, even if it was without a saddle, bridle, and reins.

Hudson bolted out of the herd and raced downriver, the horse's hooves kicking up small splashes of water. Still using the horse's mane—and his knees— he guided the animal up the bank where the Mexican officer had gone. In moments he was pounding across the plains, feeling better than he had since this mission had begun.

Within a few minutes, Hudson was closing in fast on the officer. The lieutenant seemed to know it, and he glanced over his shoulder. Knowing he could not outrun the horse, he stopped and waited, using the time to catch his breath.

Hudson stopped a few yards away and slid off the horse. He pulled his rifle off his back and set it on the ground. Tugging out his large knife, he advanced on the Mexican officer, who stood with a sword in his left hand. He did not appear to be afraid.

"You and your soldados had no call to attack my men, boy," Hudson said in English, neither knowing nor caring whether the officer understood him.

"You brought gringo soldiers into our land," the Mexican said in accented but quite good English.

"We were lookin' for some other soldiers who were taken by the Comanches."

The officer shrugged. "We're at war, our two countries."

"I ain't at war with nobody, boy," Hudson said, "'cept shit sticks who try'n kill me and take all my plunder. And Comanches who capture soldiers and innocent senoras."

"Oh?" The officer registered surprise.

"They were wives of men workin' for Bill Bent," Hudson said flatly. He paused, then decided he might as well tell the rest. "The soldiers we're lookin' for took 'em to sport with 'em across the river. That's when the Comanches grabbed 'em all. We're lookin' for the soldiers to punish 'em for takin' the women. And to pay back the Comanches for takin' 'em all."

"That means nothing to me. You brought gringo soldiers to my land. My men and I found you and made you pay the price."

"That don't shine with me, boy," Hudson spat. "Now it's your turn to pay the price."

The officer bowed his head a little, then raised it. "Try me." He whipped the sword out in front of him a couple of times in challenge.

"Don't mind if I do." Hudson slapped the flat side of his knife against his right thigh a few times. Then he and the Mexican advanced.

The officer was small and wiry, lessening the advantage of having a sword. Still, he knew how to handle the long blade.

Hudson didn't much care how good the Mexican was with the sword.

The officer feinted a few times, backing Hudson up a step or so each time. Then he lunged forward, the point of his sword reaching for Hudson's heart. Hudson dropped to the ground on his right side and swung his legs, sweeping the officer's feet out from under him. By the time the Mexican had hit the ground, Hudson was on top of him. A moment later he had plunged his blade into the officer's chest twice.

Hudson stood and wiped the knife off before sheathing it. Then he turned, got his rifle and jumped on the horse. He did not bother looking back as he rode off toward the Mexicans' camp.

CHAPTER 19

"Where'd you get off to, Linus?" Lowell asked as Hudson dismounted in the Mexican camp.

"Jist payin' my respects to the shit stick who led this group of sorry assholes," Hudson said, walking his horse toward the herd, which now was swollen with the stolen Comanche ponies.

"He still out there?" Lowell asked, falling into step beside Hudson.

"Yep. That ol' boy's worm food now. Any idea how many of 'em did git away?"

"Couldn't be more than four or five, I'd say. You figurin' to go out huntin' 'em?"

"Hell, no," Hudson snorted. "We got better things to do. Besides, they're as good as dead."

"How can you be sure of that?"

"Them ones that took off, they git away with any supplies?" Hudson countered.

"Not that we can see. I think they're lucky to have the clothes they're wearin'."

"We're maybe a hundred miles or so from the

nearest Mexican town. There ain't much water between here and there, the sun's blisterin' hot, and they got no food and water. Plus, they're on foot—in Comanche country."

Lowell nodded. His thoughts turned to when he and his men had so recently been in the same position. It was not a good position to be in but he could not find much pity in his heart for the Mexican soldiers. Not only had they attacked Lowell and his group and left them for dead, they were also the enemy of the United States. Had Lowell and his five soldiers not been sent on this mission, they would be fighting their way through the northern reaches of Mexico right now.

Hudson turned his horse out to join the herd. He called Hogg over. "Tend him good for me, Private," he said.

Hogg, not very friendly under the best of circumstances, shrugged and then look at Lowell. "That an order, Sergeant?"

"Of course."

Mumbling, Hogg shuffled off.

Turning to walk back toward the main part of the camp, Hudson said, "We'll stay here the rest of the day and the night. It'll give us a chance to see what supplies we got and let everyone rest up some. We leave in the mornin', we're gonna push it hard."

"Gettin' itchy?" Lowell almost thought it was humorous.

"No," Hudson said flatly. "I'm plumb tired of this shit. I aim to find your missin' blue coats and raise some hair on the Comanches. And I aim to git it done soon. This's dragged on far too long for this ol' boy."

Lowell nodded, suddenly infused with a good dose of Hudson's determination and annoyance at their so-far unsuccessful mission.

They pulled out in the morning just after dawn, almost overburdened with horses and supplies. They had found plenty of food, most of it dried or salted, coffee, water, and other supplies. Plus they had recovered their saddles, bridles, and other equipment.

They went east, out of the canyon and along the Canadian River. Hudson had decided that they would head toward the only place they knew the captured soldiers had been.

They left the Mexican camp with renewed spirits. The bleak, dangerous, brutally hot land no longer held any terror for the soldiers. They had faced hard times the likes of which they had never dreamed and they had come through them intact.

They moved hard and fast, changing horses when the need arose, so that they wouldn't have to stop more than occasionally. They ate their noon meals in the saddle, chewing on jerky or salted meat, and swilling water. They would camp wherever they were when darkness fell. They ate well then and in the mornings.

Hudson wasn't sure if their luck had changed for the better a little or whether it was chance or whether they were searching more intently, but they found more sign of Comanches as they rode. They also encountered more Comanche villages. They carefully scouted the villages out or sent Mad

Buffalo into them to check for the missing soldiers.

After several more days of fruitless searching, though, Hudson's mood began to sour again. When they spotted another village off in the distance, Hudson called them all to a halt behind a small ridge.

"You want me to ride in there?" Mad Buffalo asked. "Or should we poke around some?"

"Neither," Hudson said flatly. "We ain't been gittin' nowhere with such tactics."

"You got another idea?"

"Yep. Catch us a Comanche."

"What for?" Lowell asked.

"Maybe we can convince him to give us a little information that might make our searchin' easier."

Mad Buffalo was nodding. "Should've done it a long time ago."

"You sure that'll work, Linus?" Lowell asked. "What makes you think these Comanches'll know any more than the ones Mad Buffalo's talked to?"

Hudson shrugged. "I don't. But we ain't gittin' anywhere the way we been goin' about it. This don't work here, we'll try it again a few other places and see what happens."

"If you say so, Linus," Lowell said skeptically.

"Let me tell it to you this way, Sergeant—I am one powerful frustrated son of a bitch right now. We've been out here for weeks and ain't accomplished shit except to git our asses kicked by the Comanches and the fuckin' Mexicans. I aim for that to change and goddamn soon."

"You know, Linus," Lowell said thoughtfully, "I'm about as plumb annoyed at all this as you are."

He sighed in irritation. "I've been lookin' at this as just some kind of routine army duty. And maybe it was at first. But it ain't anymore. I reckon it is time to go full out."

"Glad to hear it," Hudson said dryly. But he appreciated it. "Get a man up on the top of the ridge, Sergeant. Have him keep an eye out for Comanches. I doubt they'll know we're here, but you never can be sure. If he sees a warrior movin' out this way by himself, tell him to let me know."

"Done."

It was several hours and two changes of the guards before word came that a Comanche had left the village but he was heading east.

"You and your boys stay here, Sergeant," Hudson said, hastily saddling his horse. "If the Comanches git wind of you, get your asses out of here. Keep an eye on Stolen Back Woman for me, too, if you don't mind. We'll be back as soon as we can."

"We?" Lowell asked. Then he nodded, understanding. "You and Mad Buffalo, of course."

"Yep." Hudson swung into the saddle. Then he and the Cheyenne were riding hard, heading a little northwest to keep away from the village, then swinging east a few miles away.

Hudson never ceased to be amazed at Mad Buffalo's uncanny ability to pick up a trail or to see something at great distances. So he was not surprised when Mad Buffalo stopped and pointed.

Hudson, who had far better eyesight than most men, stood in the saddle and looked. "I don't see nothin'," he said a little peevishly.

"Threequarters of a mile," Mad Buffalo said. "Heading along the front of that big ridge out there."

"I think you're full of shit," Hudson said, settling back into the saddle. He knew the Cheyenne was telling the truth and that annoyed him all the more. He sighed. "Well, let's go say hello to that shit stick."

Mad Buffalo grinned a little and kicked his pony into a trot.

They were silent in the few minutes it took to cover the distance separating them from the Comanche. The Indian seemed to suspect someone was approaching him from the rear and he turned to look back. Then he stopped and turned to face the two men approaching him.

Hudson and Mad Buffalo slowed some, then the Cheyenne held out an arm sideways, indicating that the former mountain man should stop. Hudson did and waited, Mad Buffalo stopped a few paces farther on.

The Comanche suddenly screeched a war cry and kicked his horse into motion. Mad Buffalo did the same.

Watching, Hudson thought it made a hell of a spectacle. Two young, tough warriors heading for each other at breakneck speed, howls streaming from their mouths.

Mad Buffalo suddenly jammed to a halt and thrust his lance at the Comanche, who blocked it with his war shield. He took a stab at Mad Buffalo with his own lance, but the Cheyenne knocked it out of the way with his spear. Then Mad Buffalo spun his lance and smashed the Comanche across the face with it. The Comanche fell off his horse and bounced in the dust.

Mad Buffalo jumped off his pony. As the Comanche tried to get up, Mad Buffalo slammed him in the face again with the haft of his spear. The Comanche didn't go out, but he was mighty groggy. Mad Buffalo dropped his lance and sliced a few thongs from the Comanche's buckskin leggings. He used the pieces to bind the Comanche's hands behind his back. Then he grabbed the enemy's hair and jerked him to his feet.

The Comanche wavered a little but then steadied himself. Hudson trotted up with the Comanche's horse, which had run off a little ways when its rider had fallen.

"Get up there," Mad Buffalo said in sign language. He helped the bound Indian onto his pony, then mounted his own horse.

Hudson moved up with a rope and placed a slip knotted loop around the Comanche's neck. He looped the other end of the rope around his saddle horn, and the three moved off.

They took a circuitous route back to where the others were waiting. Lowell reported that they had seen nothing untoward about the village, which still seemed to be oblivious to their being there.

"Let's put some distance between ourselves and that goddamn village," Hudson said.

Ten miles and a few hours later, they stopped along a creek that was mostly dry. It was almost dark and the men hurried to get their tasks done so they could eat. As soon as they stopped, Hudson pulled the Comanche none too gently down from the pony. He bound him well to a small, stunted tree and then went about his business.

They ate well and then turned in almost immediately after. Hudson gave no food to their prisoner, figuring that might help soften him up for questioning later. The Comanche was given no food in the morning either. Hudson and Mad Buffalo sat at the morning fire, eating well, keeping their eyes on the Comanche. Then they took their time dawdling over coffee and pipes, still watching the prisoner.

"He don't look like he'll be easy to get to talk," Lowell said noncommittally.

"He'll talk," Hudson said evenly.

"I don't doubt it, but it's gonna take a while, I expect."

Hudson nodded. "It might not be pretty, Sergeant," he said flatly. "If you and your boys'd prefer moseyin' on a little ways to wait, I'll understand."

"Nope," Lowell said firmly. "If you and Mad Buffalo can stand to do it, me and the boys can stand to watch it." He grinned ruefully and added, "I hope."

Finally, Hudson and Mad Buffalo stood and headed toward the Comanche. The soldiers tentatively followed. Hudson and the Cheyenne squatted in front of the prisoner. "You speak English, boy?" Hudson asked.

When the Indian continued to stare blankly at him, Hudson asked in Cheyenne, "Do you speak Cheyenne?"

Still the vacant look remained.

Hudson shrugged. He could use sign language as well as any Comanche. It would have to suffice here. Using the signs, he asked, "Have you seen any blue coats in the past few weeks?"

The Comanche said nothing. His face was impassive.

"You're making this hard on yourself," Hudson signed. "All we want is some information. You give it to us, you can go back to your people in peace."

Still nothing.

Hudson looked at Mad Buffalo. "I'm tired of this shit already," he said in English.

Mad Buffalo nodded.

Hudson pulled his knife and slit through the Comanche's right legging. Then he punched the knife tip into the captive's thigh just a little. He slid the knife down the leg, leaving behind a thin trail of blood. As he worked, he talked in English, directing his comments to the Comanche. "It's been a time since I skinned me anyone. I ain't so sure I still got the knack of it."

"It'll come back to ya," Mad Buffalo said encouragingly, also in English.

Hudson stuck the knife into the leg again, about two inches to the right of the first incision. He drew it down again and then cut across the ending to the other cut. He carefully poked the knife into the small slit, prying up just the top layer of skin. When he had some loose, he grabbed it with his fingers and then began peeling it back along the incisions.

The captive made no sound and showed no signs of pain. He did glare in hate at the white man and the Cheyenne.

Hudson moved to the other leg and did the same thing. Then he pulled another strip of skin from that leg and then again. He returned to the first one and stripped more skin off, his movements deft and sure.

All it got him was more glaring and no sound.

Hudson had expected the Comanche to be hardened to this and for it to have little effect, but he thought it necessary to show the prisoner that he could do it—and therefore, by extension, much worse. But he was tiring of the game already. "I'll ask you this one more time," he signed. "Have you seen any blue coats in the past few weeks?"

When the Comanche still said nothing, Hudson called over his shoulder, "Stolen Back Woman, come here, woman." He handed her the knife as she knelt between Hudson and Mad Buffalo. Hudson looked at the Comanche. "This is my woman," he signed. "A fine woman of the Cheyenne people. I will have her take your manhood while you sit and watch it happen. Then she'll take you hair."

The words seemed to have little effect on the captive. "After that, me'n Mad Buffalo here'll kill you, slowly and with much pain. And then we'll leave you here to be picked over by the wolves and coyotes and buzzards. Since you won't be a whole man no more and you won't have your scalp, you won't get into the spirit world. You'll wander for all eternity."

"I'm not afraid," the prisoner said in Comanche. Since his hands were tied behind his back and the tree, he could not use signs. He almost didn't care whether these men understood him.

Hudson understood enough. He didn't know much Comanche, but he did know enough for simple sentences. "Maybe you're not afraid," he said with signs. "But your wanderin' spirit ain't gonna be happy. And worse, adding to the insult we place on you, your cherished hair and your manhood will be taken by a woman. Not even by a warrior on the field of battle. The spirits'll piss on you."

The Comanche thought that over for some moments, then nodded his head. What the white man had threatened had little meaning to him. Nor did it instill fear in him. Still, he figured that if he acted a little like it did, he might find a way to escape and wreak havoc with these enemies. His medicine was strong and would see him through this little problem.

"I'll talk," he said in Comanche. "Loosen my hands so I might talk in signs." He was almost contemptuous, figuring that the white man knew little of his language.

CHAPTER 20

"First thing, what's your name, boy?" Hudson asked.

"I am the Taker of the Horses," the Comanche said with pride. He used signs but also spoke in his own language.

Hudson nodded. "Now tell it," he said with signs. He knew only a few words of the Comanche language and he suspected Horse Taker was insulting him and Mad Buffalo with his words while "talking" properly in signs. He didn't much care at the moment.

"I don't know much about these men you seek," Horse Taker said in signs. "Some of our brothers came to our village with three blue coats. They stayed only a short time. Then they left."

"That doesn't tell me much," Hudson signed. He let his face show his displeasure at Horse Taker's unwillingness to offer information.

"We tested the blue coats' courage some," Horse Taker said in signs. "They were stronger than I thought they'd be. Then the People celebrated with the visitors. We had a dance and a feast."

"And?" Hudson queried, irritated.

"And then our brothers went away. They took the blue coats with them."

"Then the blue coats are alive?" Hudson asked. He figured they must have been, considering most Indians' fear of the dead. Still, he had to be sure.

Horse Taker nodded.

Hudson tried not to let his relief show. "Where'd they go?" he asked, still using signs.

Horse Taker shrugged, showing his disinterest.

Hudson squatted silently for a moment, straining to control a burst of anger. Then he said, with signs, "Your wellbeing in the afterlife is still in my hands. If you don't cooperate more, I'll do what I warned." He was not sure whether the threat would continue to have any effect on the Comanche.

Horse Taker shrugged again. "If I talk more, you'll still do those things to me," he signed. "If I must die and my spirit wander, or go to the afterworld as less than a man, there's no reason to say more." He crossed his arms over his chest with finality. He was not worried. The enemy had threatened to do those things to him while he was alive. If that happened, it would not affect his entrance into the afterworld. He was certain that this white man did not know that.

"I won't do those things if you talk," Hudson signed. "I give my word."

Horse Taker spit in contempt. "The word of a white eye is worth less than the dung of a dog," he signed, face still showing his derision.

Hudson stroked his stubbled chin. He knew full well that a Comanche warrior, or any other warrior he had encountered, could endure extremes of pain, and would die without offering another piece of information, if he put his mind to it. Hudson knew he could peel all the skin from Horse Taker's hide or beat him to death without the Comanche saying anything more. That would not help the mission the white men were on here. He had hoped to use the Comanche's natural fear of the afterlife and the way he would enter it against him, but that did not seem to be working. Hudson wasn't sure why.

Hudson knew that what he needed to do was somehow break Horse Taker's medicine. Trouble was, he didn't know how to go about that. Not without knowing the Comanche's history, his visions, his life, something that would give him a clue into Horse Taker's taboos and spirit powers.

While Hudson was still pondering what to do, Mad Buffalo, who was squatting next to him, began speaking to Horse Taker, using Comanche. The words had little effect for a minute, but then Horse Taker's face began to show some worry and fear. The more Mad Buffalo talked, the worse the Comanche seemed to get. Finally, after just a few minutes, Mad Buffalo ground to a halt.

Obviously shaken, Horse Taker looked at Hudson. "You will not take my hair or... anything else?" he asked.

"No."

"You won't choke me to death?"

"No," Hudson signed, a little surprised.

"I spoke the truth before," Horse Taker said with signs. He had stopped speaking in Comanche while signing. "I don't know much. When our cousins left, they said they planned to hunt buffalo to the north, maybe with our friends the Kiowas. Then they were going to meet their own band in Palo Duro Canyon."

Hudson nodded and looked at Mad Buffalo. "Think he's tellin' true?"

Mad Buffalo simply nodded.

Hudson was a little surprised, but he accepted it. "Did those warriors have women with them?" he asked. "Mexican women?"

"No. They said they had captured three such women with the blue coats. Our cousins gave the women to another band, east of here."

Hudson let that settle in his brain a moment. He was more than a little surprised that the women were still alive, or at least had been a few days ago. He had figured the warriors who had captured them would have used them mercilessly and then killed them, as they had the one whose remains Mad Buffalo had found.

Now he was in a quandary. He felt he owed it to Bill Bent to try to rescue the women. However, even though the village where the women had been left, if Horse Taker was speaking the truth, was in the direction of Palo Duro Canyon, it would take time to find a village. It would take still more time to ascertain whether the women were in that village. If not, they would have to search some more, much as they had done in the past two weeks. The more time they spent in such doings, would mean the longer the soldiers would be in the clutches of the Comanches.

The latter worried Hudson some. He had a hunch

that Palo Duro Canyon was the destination of the Comanche war party. If true, it might mean that the soldiers didn't have much longer to live. That lent a certain amount of urgency to their mission.

"So, what do we do, Fierce Bear?" Mad Buffalo asked. "Head for the canyon?"

"No," Hudson said after only a moment's hesitation. "We go for the women first."

"That could be dangerous—for the blue coats."

"Yep, it could. But I owe it to Bill to try'n fetch the women back. To tell you the truth, I don't much give a shit about the soldiers. It wasn't for them, we wouldn't be out here, and Whirlin' Storm'd still be alive."

"Might take some huntin' to find 'em," Mad Buffalo pressed.

Hudson grinned tightly. "I got faith in your abilities, boy."

"What about him?" Mad Buffalo asked, pointing to Horse Taker.

"Tie his arms back up and leave him here."

Mad Buffalo nodded. "That shines. You gonna leave him his hair and all, though?"

"I said I would." The tight grin grew almost vicious. "I didn't say I wouldn't leave him out here for the scavengers to tear apart. I don't expect that shit stick's gonna make it to the afterworld in one piece."

"That don't worry me."

"Bind him up good. I want to be on the trail as soon as we can."

As Mad Buffalo went to tie Horse Taker's arms

behind him again, Hudson went about getting the others moving. Since Lowell had already had his men saddle and bridle the horses, it was only a matter of minutes before everyone was mounted and they were moving out.

Hudson looked back only once and could see the buzzards circling over the Comanche already. He nodded. "It ain't much to avenge your spirit, Whirlin' Storm," he muttered, "but it's a start."

Just after leaving, before Mad Buffalo had moved out into his scouting position, Hudson pulled him aside and asked, "Jist what did you say to that shit stick to oil up his tongue? I figured for sure he wasn't gonna say another goddamn word to us."

Mad Buffalo grinned a little. "I know a bit more about his people than you do and so I know some of their secrets. I could see that your threats to have Stolen Back Woman carve him up didn't mean much to him, so I added somethin' I figured would do the job."

"And what was that?"

"I told him that Stolen Back Woman was unclean."

Hudson nodded, understanding. All male Indians he knew of were troubled, worried, and even frightened by a menstruating woman. Such a statement from Mad Buffalo would've put the fear of all kinds of spirits in Horse Taker's mind. Then something dawned on him. "She ain't in that time," he said.

"He didn't know that," Mad Buffalo said with a small laugh.

"Goddamn, you're one sneaky ol' bastard, ain't

you."

"Yep. Since I wasn't sure that was gonna work, though, I also told him that Stolen Back Woman was carryin' his war shield."

"Their war shields are mighty special to the Comanches, aren't they?"

"Yep. It's a Comanche warrior's most important possession. For an unclean woman to handle a Comanche's war shield is about the worst thing that could happen to his medicine."

"Seems to've worked."

"Yep. I threw in a few more things for him to consider, too," Mad Buffalo said. He seemed to be getting a considerable amount of enjoyment out of this. "Like tellin' him we would put him under by stranglin' him and that we'd do it after dark."

"More worries from the spirits?"

"Yep. Comanches believe that goin' under from bein' strangled won't let their spirit free. They think the spirit comes out of the mouth when they die," he said almost contemptuously. "Close off the air passage and the spirit ain't got any way of gittin' out"

"And night?"

"Comanches're afraid that if they die in the darkness, their spirit won't be able to find out where the hell it's goin' and they won't be able to find the afterworld."

"Goddamn, boy, you're even sneakier'n I thought," Hudson said in pride.

"I learned it all from you," Mad Buffalo1 said with a grin. He kicked his pony and galloped off.

As they had done earlier, Hudson and the

soldiers kept watch from a little distance from the village, while Mad Buffalo rode in, pretending to be hunting or visiting or whatever he thought the Comanches wanted to hear. Once in the village, the Cheyenne would poke around as much as he could without raising suspicion, looking for the captive Mexican women.

It was not until the fourth village, though, that they had some success. By then, Hudson was swamped with frustration again and was nearly ready to call off the search for the women and just head for Palo Duro Canyon. Still, they had come this far, and Hudson was reluctant to give up searching for the women just yet.

Then Mad Buffalo had ridden into another village. He was there overnight, causing Hudson some worry. But just after dawn, Mad Buffalo rode slowly out of the village, looking for all the world as if he had not a care in the world. Once behind the ridge with his friends, he dismounted and nodded. 'They're there," he announced.

Hudson, who had been about to berate the Cheyenne, clamped off the harsh words. "You're sure?"

Mad Buffalo looked at his friend as if he had gone mad.

"Christ, all right, it was a damn fool question," Hudson said with a laugh. Then he grew serious. "They all right?" he asked.

Mad Buffalo nodded. "I reckon. I couldn't talk to 'em, but they seemed to be all right but beaten down."

Hudson accepted the information. After a few minutes of thought, he nodded. "I'll go fetch 'em this afternoon," he announced.

"How the hell're you gonna do that?" Lowell asked, surprised.

"I got me a plan. You jist keep your men here and watch over the animals. Mad Buffalo'll be here in case somethin' happens. If it does, you listen to him. He knows the way of things."

"But..." Lowell shut up, knowing he had nothing of importance to say.

For the next several hours, Hudson and Mad Buffalo huddled together, talking quietly. Stolen Back Woman was quietly solicitous of them, though they had no fires, so there was no hot food and no coffee. The soldiers took turns keeping watch from the crest of the ridge. Finally, Hudson and Mad Buffalo began loading some of the group's supplies on the few mules they had.

Just after noon, Hudson headed toward the Comanche village. He showed no fear as several warriors rode out and surrounded him. "I come from the big adobe lodge on the Arkansas," he said with signs. "I come to trade with the Comanches."

A scarred faced warrior looked at him with little disguised disgust. Then he nodded. "I'm Buffalo Back," he said. "Come."

Minutes later they were in the village and Hudson was talking with Yellow Rock, one of the main chiefs of the village. Hudson was sweating from the heat, as well as from a desire to get this done with. He passed around a few gifts of small trinkets—the group had little in the way of trade goods, so he didn't have much to work with—and then casually asked if there were any captives in the camp. He and the Comanches spoke with signs.

"Captives?" Yellow Rock asked.

"A couple of Mexican women were taken from the adobe lodge by Apaches," he lied easily. "I heard that the captives ended up with a Comanche band. Probably because the Comanches kicked the Apaches' asses and took the women." He wanted to vomit at having to kowtow to the Comanches like this.

"Such may be true," Yellow Rock said slowly. "But what does that have to do with me?"

"The chief of the adobe lodge would like them back. If you have them, he would pay well for their return."

Yellow Rock appeared to think that over for a while. "What will you give me for them?" he finally asked. "If they are here," he added.

"I have little to give now," Hudson signed, face impassive. "But the chief of the adobe lodge will give Yellow Rock many presents the next time the great Comanche chief goes there. This I promise you. And this he will promise you."

"How can I trust the word of the white eyes?" Yellow Rock asked harshly.

"The chief of the adobe lodge has traded with the Comanches for many years. He has always been fair and truthful with your people. He won't change now. Not when he wants the women back very much."

"Why does he want these women? Mexican

women are easy to find. He could have more. Many more. As many as he wants."

"They are the women of some of his workers and so they are special to him. Like they were his daughters."

Yellow Rock fell silent. Then he nodded. "You will give me what trade goods you have," he said with signs. "And you will tell the adobe chief that he will give us many gifts when we visit his lodge." There was finality in his voice.

"I have few trade goods, but I'll give you what I have. And the fort chief will pay well when you go there."

"It is good," Yellow Rock signed. He paused, then said, "I'll take the two extra horses you have, too."

"Shit," Hudson breathed. Still, it was a cheap way of getting out of this. He nodded and signed, "It is good."

Yellow Rock smiled. Then he pulled out a ceremonial pipe and the two men smoked to seal their pact.

Hudson could not believe how easy this had been and he worried that something might yet go wrong. He smoked calmly, though, despite his eagerness to get the women and leave the village.

Finally, though, Yellow Rock called for the women to be brought. Hudson stood and took what trade goods he had from his mules and set the items down in front of Yellow Rock.

CHAPTER 21

Hudson kept his face impassive when the women arrived. Both were in their mid to late twenties, and might have been pretty were it not for their bruised faces and the downtrodden looks they wore. Their long, dark hair was matted and dirty, their clothes tattered and filthy. Both looked at the ground, refusing to lift their eyes. They had been humiliated beyond all belief and did not want to look at anyone—or to have anyone look into their eyes and see the debasement there.

"Don't you two think of what's gone on," Hudson said quietly as he walked between the two to get the last of the trade goods. On the way back, he said, "You'll be all right now." He didn't think he had convinced them of that. Hell, he wasn't even sure they understood much English. He hoped the words or at least his voice, reassured them a little.

He approached them again and said in a soft, but urgent voice, "Git on the mules, senoras. Pronto!" When they seemed reluctant—or maybe just unable—to move, Hudson grabbed each one by a shoulder, gently turned them and nudged them toward the mules. "Best move it some, senoras," he said, "lest these boys change their minds." He was having serious doubts that they understood him or could function.

But his last words seemed to galvanize the two women. Still, with heads down, they moved to mules and pulled themselves on.

With a sigh of relief, Hudson mounted his horse. "Adios," he said with a wave at Yellow Horse. "Go on, senoras," he said, wanting them to be ahead of him when they left the village. Then, towing his two remaining mules behind him, he rode out of the village.

Hudson kept a watch behind him as they went. Less than three hundred yards past the last of the lodges, he spotted four Comanches racing toward him and the women. "Ride hard!" he shouted.

The two women looked back, faces showing no fear, only the dullness of defeat. But they kicked their mules into hurrying. It was as if they didn't really expect to be free but suddenly realized that they might have a chance—if they could get away from the charging warriors.

Hudson galloped after them, the extra mules behind. He kept looking back and cursed when he saw how swiftly the Comanches were closing the distance. Finally, Hudson pulled to a stop, letting the two extra mules continue running, following the two women mounted on other mules.

He pulled his rifle from the rawhide loop on the

front of his saddle. He dismounted, knelt, aimed, and fired, all within seconds. One of the Comanches toppled off his horse.

The other warriors howled and pressed even harder. Hudson swept into the saddle, slid the rifle back into the rawhide loop, and pulled his Colt Patersons. An arrow carried off his felt hat, causing him more annoyance than anything else. He was not surprised, though, that they were shooting high. He figured they wanted to kill him and take his horse and so would not risk hitting the animal. Unless, of course, things started going bad for them.

Other arrows arced his way as the Comanches closed in. With a shrug, Hudson rode toward the warriors, ignoring the raining arrows. He was little surprised that none of the shafts hit him, since he had his own medicine and it was as powerful, he felt, as any the Comanches could come up with.

When he was less than fifty yards from one warrior, who was slightly ahead of his fellows, Hudson opened fire with one pistol, firing twice. The first Comanche went down, as if he had been jerked off his pony.

Then a second warrior was on him and Hudson fired the last two shots in his pistol. They seemed to have no effect on the warrior, who clubbed him down off his horse with his lance.

Hudson landed on his side, getting the breath knocked out of him for a moment. As he began getting up, he hoped nothing had been broken or damaged inside. He got to his feet, eyes swiftly sweeping the ground as he looked for his pistols. A bow cracked him across the top of the back, and he went down again, landing on his face.

As he got up again, pain clutched at his back and side. He took a hasty glance around and noted that the two Comanches had stopped a few yards away, one to his left, one to his right. They were taunting him. Hudson couldn't understand their words, but the meaning was clear enough.

"Suck wind, you dickless shit sticks," he roared back. Facing one Comanche, he grabbed his crotch and thrust his groin at him. Then he bent and wiggled his buttocks at the other. "Chew on that, goddamn you," he said.

He smiled when he saw irritation flicker across one warrior's face. Using hand signs, he called the Comanche in front of him a coward and impugned the Indian's ancestry.

The Comanche let loose a bloodcurdling war cry and charged, still on horseback.

As he began pulling out his tomahawk, Hudson suddenly spotted his two pistols. One was almost at his feet, the other several feet away. He hoped the nearest one was the loaded one. He knelt and scooped the pistol up, and realized that the Comanche who had been behind him had just tried to whack him with his bow again. The weapon passed a few inches over Hudson's head.

"Dickless bastard," Hudson shouted as he shoved to his feet. He thumbed back the revolver's hammer and fired. Nothing happened. He tried twice more, each time with the same result. "Fuck," he mumbled. He threw the useless pistol aside and dove for the other revolver. As he grabbed it and started to rise, cocking the gun, he heard a shout. He spun and saw Mad Buffalo just braining one of the Comanches, splitting the warrior's skull with his tomahawk.

Hudson spun back toward the other Comanche, who was now racing toward the village. Hudson emptied his revolver at the fleeing warrior but did not hit him. A moment later, though, Mad Buffalo was charging after the Comanche, rapidly catching up.

Mad Buffalo put two arrows in the enemy's back. The Comanche fell, but his pony continued running. Mad Buffalo stopped and slid off his horse. Within a moment, he had peeled the Comanche's scalp and then jumped on his pony.

"Saved your ass again, white eye," Mad Buffalo said as he stopped near Hudson.

The former mountain man was reloading one of his Colts. "Jist saved me the trouble of havin' to kill more Comanches," Hudson grumbled. He wasn't really angry. He had saved Mad Buffalo's life enough times and vice versa. He was just irritated at the situation as a whole.

"Next time I'll jist set and watch," Mad Buffalo said. He hopped off his pony and pulled his knife. "You want any of their hair?" he asked.

"Got no use for such," he said, sticking the one Colt in his belt and bending to pick up the other one. "But if you're too goddamn squeamish to raise hair on these boys, I'll do it jist so they don't git to the Happy Huntin' Ground."

Mad Buffalo ignored the latter statement. "We might have a use for 'em," he said.

"What's that?"

"When we find the Comanches holdin' the blue coats, we might use these scalps to break the medicine of those Comanches."

"Can't hurt to try," Hudson said thoughtfully. "All right, we'll bring 'em."

While Mad Buffalo hurried to take the three other scalps, Hudson finished reloading his second revolver. Then he mounted his horse and hurriedly gathered up the two Comanche ponies that had remained behind. The fourth had drifted back toward the village.

Hudson and his Cheyenne friend rode hard for the ridge where the soldiers and the others were. Once there, they did not even dismount. "We best git the hell out of here," he announced. "Pronto."

"Comanches comin?" Lowell asked. He seemed unfazed by the possibility.

"Nope. But there's no tellin' how those shit sticks're gonna react once they find out me and Mad Buffalo rubbed out four of their warriors."

"Enough said," Lowell responded with a tight nod. "Let's go, men. Private O'Murray, you and Private Hochner help the Mexican women onto horses. Not mules. Move it!"

The last warning was not needed. Everyone was moving already and doing so swiftly. Stolen Back Woman had mounted her pony and had ridden to Hudson's side.

He smiled at her, leaned over and touched her cheek. "Miss me, woman?" he asked softly.

"Always," Stolen Back Woman responded without

shame or embarrassment.

"I reckon you're sorry you come chasin' after me, though," he said with a grin.

The Cheyenne shook her head. She lived with danger every day of her life. This wasn't much different, other than there was more traveling and the danger might be compressed into a smaller time period. As long as she was with her man, she thought she was doing fine.

They pulled out, Mad Buffalo leading the way eastward. They moved at a pretty good pace, wanting to put some distance between themselves and the Comanche village. As they rode, Lowell moved up alongside Hudson. "You have any trouble gettin' the women out?" he asked. "Other than that fight at the end there."

"Nope. Hell, I was thinkin' to myself jist after I pulled out of there that things were goin' a mite too smooth. It jist seemed so easy. I figured somethin' was gonna go wrong, which it finally did. I think that shit stick Yellow Rock planned to send those boys out after me and the women all along."

"Who's Yellow Rock?"

"The dickless chief I dealt with back there. I think he figured he'd lull me into thinkin' everything was cozy 'tween me'n his people. That part worked well enough, dammit," Hudson said, anger at himself rising. "Son of a bitch, if that don't piss me off." He took a moment to let the anger settle down some. "Anyway, he probably figured he could have it all, the son of a bitch. He could git my hair, the mules, the women back, have his men count coup, plus still git

Bill to give him a passel of goods the next time that disease drippin' old fart went to Bent's."

"Sounds logical," Lowell said thoughtfully. "Except for the last. What would make him think he could get a load of goods at Bent's?"

"I told him he could. I didn't have enough trade goods to ransom those women, so I told him that Bill'd be glad to pay him a heap. If Yellow Rock had kept his word, I would've, too. Trouble is, I think that old bastard planned that in there, too. I'd told him that Bill really wanted the women back. I suppose dripping dick there figured that once he killed me and got the women back, he could mosey up to Bent's place himself and ransom the women there. Connivin' sack of shit."

"He sure sounds like one," Lowell agreed. "Do you think he'll send his men after us?"

"Doubt it. First off, like most Injins out here, he cain't send any warriors anywhere. He might call for a war party, though I don't think that's likely either. Once me'n Mad Buffalo killed four warriors from his village and raised their hair so they can't get into the afterworld, there's every chance that goddamn Yellow Rock'll figure not only his but the whole damned village's medicine's gone plumb bad. He'll want to make more medicine before he'd want to risk another battle with a white man."

"Then why push so hard?" Lowell was still sore of rump from all the riding they had done.

"Considerin' how sneaky that shit stick is," Hudson growled, "I cain't be absolute positive jist what he will or won't do. He jist might be crazy enough to think his medicine's strong enough to allow him and some chosen men—also with strong medicine—take us. So, goddammit, we ride hard."

And ride they did. Hudson stopped them around midnight and again just after dawn to give the horses a rest. The first time, they could not chance a fire, so they ate jerked meat and drank water. In the daylight, though, they could see that no one was following them, so Hudson allowed fires. Mad Buffalo brought in two antelope, so they ate well. Hot coffee also served to revive them.

The two senoras ate at Hudson's fire with the former mountain man, Mad Buffalo, Lowell, and Stolen Back Woman. "What're your names, senoras?" Lowell asked, trying to draw the two women out a little.

"I'm Lourdes Garda," one finally got the courage to say meekly. She nodded at the other woman. "And she's Guadalupe Sanchez."

"Pleased to meet you," Lowell said with his usual civility.

The two women said nothing, but they nodded. They ate in silence for a while before Lourdes said, in heavily accented English, "Thank you, senor, for helping us." She was looking at the former mountain man, but her gaze swiftly fell back to the ground.

Hudson shrugged. "Bill Bent wanted me to bring you back, if I could," he said lamely.

"How long will it be before we get back there?" the same woman asked.

"It'll be a while, senora," Hudson said. "We got other business to tend to before we head to Bent's."

"What business?" the woman asked, face blanching. She was afraid to ask, lest these men get angry at her. She was also afraid to hear the answer.

"There's a couple of soldiers out here bein' held captive by the Comanches," Hudson said flatly. "We got to go fetch 'em back for the army."

Lourdes's face grew even more pale. "But they... they..."

"I know what they done to you and your friend, senora. But I'll tell you right here and now, that they ain't gonna pull no such doin's again. The army wants 'em back to punish 'em. They even look at you or Senora Sanchez crossways and I'll personally see that they lose all interest in all women for all time. Same goes for any of the men here. My meanin' clear?"

Guadalupe looked at Lourdes, and the two women spoke in rapid, fear-tinged Spanish for a few minutes. Then Lourdes nodded. "Si'," she said quietly. She paused, then added, "But we're still afraid."

"Ain't no harm in that, Senora Garcia. Not after what you and Senora Sanchez've been through. And you have reason to be scared, too, by the fact that I cain't guarantee we're any of us gonna git back to Senor Bent's. I aim to do all in my power to see that we do, though."

Lourdes nodded. She was still horrified by what had happened to her, frightened to death of what might still happen and even more fearful of the reception she and her friend would get when they returned to Bent's Fort, if they ever made it. She was sure her husband would have nothing to do with her any longer. And who could blame him? Why should any man have to live with such shame and disgust? Still, things were better now than they were a day ago and each day might get better yet. She could still hope in her heart that it would happen that way.

An hour later Hudson had them all back in the saddle and riding eastward again. He slowed the pace considerably. Late in the morning, they carefully gave another Comanche village a wide berth, then pushed on. An hour or so before dusk, Mad Buffalo led them to a sheltered spot along an almost dry creek. After their chores were done, nearly everyone in the group collapsed and slept.

CHAPTER 22

Late the next morning, Hudson and his people arrived at the ragged slash of a canyon in far upper Texas. They rode just south of a tall, wind-blasted peak. Minutes later they were on a large mesa, with the canyon spread out to their left.

Everyone was still exhausted from the past couple of days, but Hudson would not let them stop now that they were so close to their quarry—if Horse Taker had told them the truth.

Hudson and Mad Buffalo rode in single file along the rim of Mesquite Mesa, looking down the sheer cliffs into the canyon. They could see the glimmering ribbon of the Prairie Dog Town Fork of the Red River across the canyon from the mesa on which they were traveling. The others rode some yards away from the sharp canyon rim, keeping away from both the danger of the rim and the prying eyes of any Comanche who might be looking up that way. Two men might not be seen so easily from a great distance but an entire group might be another story.

Finally, Hudson, who was in the lead, stopped and pointed.

"I see it," Mad Buffalo said. Across the canyon, in a sharp bend of Prairie Dog Fork, was a Comanche village. "Might not be the right one, though."

"I know. But we got to stop and check." He wouldn't admit it, but he was worried that Horse Taker had sent them on a wild goose chase. Since Palo Duro Canyon was a favorite spot for most of the Comanche bands, the captive warrior would've figured that there would be at least one village here. He might've also thought that once Hudson, Mad Buffalo, and the soldiers got to poking around, the warriors in the canyon would get stirred up and annihilate them. It was all too real a possibility.

The two men trotted over to the others and had them make a cold camp on the barren mesa top, well back from the canyon rim. "You best git some sleep, Mad Buffler," Hudson said. "I'll watch for a while."

The Cheyenne nodded, not about to argue.

"Sergeant, post two guards. The women and the other men can get some rest. You, too. Change the guards after a couple of hours. Before that, though, you best tend the horses. They've been hard used and we may need to run 'em hard again at any time.

"Anything else I—we—can do, Linus?"

"Nope. Jist make sure the women're safe and the animals don't wander off."

Hudson pulled a collapsible telescope from the possibles bag hanging from his saddle. Stolen Back Woman handed him a buckskin satchel containing jerky and a canteen. "You have 'baccy?" she asked.

"And matches?"

"Yep. You watch over them Mexican women now, you hear me?" he said, not at all sternly. "If they'll let you."

"I'll try." Stolen Back Woman looked doubtful. She had made a few friendly overtures toward Lourdes and Guadalupe, but the Mexicans had rebuffed them, looking startled, frightened, and disgusted.

"I know they ain't gonna be fond of you, woman," Hudson said. He had seen the Mexicans rejected Stolen Back Woman. "Hell, they look at all Injins with suspicion now. It don't make no difference to 'em that you're one of the People and the ones who held 'em are Comanches."

"I know. I said I'll try."

"Ain't too many people can resist you, woman, when you set out to charm 'em," he said, smiling. He kissed her lightly. "I'll be back by dark." He walked off on foot, rifle and sack in his left hand, telescope in his right. There was almost no vegetation on the mesa top, except for sage—and one wind twisted, skeleton-like mesquite tree right on the edge of the cliff, jutting out on a small promontory.

Hudson headed for the dead tree. He leaned his rifle against it, dropped his small sack and tossed his hat on top of that. Then he plopped down on the mesa side of the tree and pulled his telescope open. Since the sun was to the south, it was at his back. He would not have to worry about the Comanches seeing any reflection from the telescope or his rifle. He peered through the scope.

After just a minute, though, he set the telescope

down. He pulled out his canteen and poured a little over his head. He wiped the water around his face, feeling the gritty tiredness in his eyes. Then he put the canteen away and went back to watching the village through his telescope.

It was a long afternoon for Hudson. He was tired and frequently had to jerk himself awake as he felt himself dozing off. Squinting through the small eyepiece of the telescope didn't help much. Nor did the heat or the boredom. Or the frustration, irritation, and anger.

Near the middle of the afternoon, Hudson suddenly snapped to alertness. He focused in on an army blouse, but it quickly became obvious that the man wearing it was a Comanche. Still, the uniform coat was the same as that worn by the soldiers accompanying Hudson.

Soon after, he spotted another Comanche wearing a soldier's coat. The two sightings were both encouraging and worrisome. It could very well mean the soldiers were there and the Indians had simply appropriated what parts of the men's uniforms they fancied. It could just as easily mean, however, that the warriors had taken the uniforms from the bodies of the troops somewhere along the trail.

Mad Buffalo strolled up after a little and squatted next to Hudson, who looked at his friend. The Cheyenne's eyes were puffy and his face slack. He had slept some, but not nearly enough.

"Christ, boy, I hope I don't look as bad as you," Hudson said.

"You always have anyway," Mad Buffalo growled.

"You see anything down there?"

Hudson explained it.

Mad Buffalo nodded, also realizing the possibilities here. "Want me to take over for a spell?" he asked.

"Hell, yes." He handed the Cheyenne the telescope and moved aside a little. He knelt there rubbing his eyes.

"You best git some sleep, my friend," Mad Buffalo said as he looked through the scope. "If they are in that village, alive, we're gonna have to go down there sometime after dark."

"Yes, mother," Hudson said a little sarcastically. He pushed himself wearily to his feet and grabbed his rifle and sack. "But you're right. Christ, I ain't been this tired in a long spell."

Hudson shuffled back to the camp. Lying on his and Stolen Back Woman's buffalo sleeping robes, he rested his head on another robe. Stolen Back Woman sat behind him, her fingers rubbing practiced circles on his forehead, temples, and cheeks. "You're too good to me, woman," Hudson mumbled, then he fell asleep.

Stolen Back Woman woke Hudson with a strong, insistent kiss. His eyes popped open, instantly alert. Stolen Back Woman pulled her head back a couple of inches. "Time to git up," she whispered.

"Something wrong?" Hudson asked.

"You have work to do."

When Stolen Back Woman moved back, Hudson sat up, rubbing his eyes. He was still beat, but he felt a little better than he had before. He looked up at the sky and judged it to be about midnight. "Where's Mad Buffler?" he asked Stolen Back Woman.

"Right here," the Cheyenne warrior responded. He had been sitting there silently all along. Now that Hudson's eyes had adjusted a little he could see his friend's dark outline. Hudson took the jerky Stolen Back Woman handed him and shoved some into his mouth. While chewing, he asked, "I take it you learned somethin', Mad Buffler." It was as much a statement as a question.

"The blue coats're there. I saw 'em."

"How'd they look?"

"Couldn't tell. Too far. They're alive and on their feet though."

"You sure it was them?"

"Nope. But there ain't been any other white eyes captured by the Comanches that I know of."

Hudson ate a little more. Then he said, "So we go down there now and fetch 'em out of there."

"Yep."

"I'll be ready in a minute," Hudson said, bolting his food down. "Does Sergeant Lowell know?"

"I do," Lowell said from behind Hudson.

"He's goin' with us, Fierce Bear," Mad Buffalo said.

"No. I want him up here to keep an eye on things."

"That ain't necessary," Mad Buffalo said.

"The hell it ain't. He's about the only one I can trust around here."

"That's bullshit, Linus," Lowell said a little heatedly. "Private O'Murray's a good man. So's Private Hochner. They'll keep an eye on things."

When Hudson didn't say anything right away, Mad Buffalo offered, "We need him with us, Fierce Bear."

"What for?"

"You think those blue coats'll be willin' to walk out of camp with another Injin and a crazy white eye they don't know and probably don't want to?"

"That would present a problem, wouldn't it," Hudson said dryly. He cranked his head around. "Be glad to have you along, Sergeant," he said. "I'd like you to remember, though, that I opposed your comin' along not because I was against you."

"I know, Linus. I also know that I'll be somewhat of a disadvantage to you and Mad Buffalo down there. I'm not accustomed to such things. But I'll do my damnedest to make you proud of me."

"I expect you will." Hudson finished his meal and gulped down a couple mouthfuls of water. "You boys ready?" he asked. When he got two affirmatives, he asked, "The guards set and all, Sergeant?"

"Everything's taken care of." Lowell was tense, a little afraid of what the night would bring, but eager to get on with it.

"You got two pistols, Sergeant?"

"No, but I will have in a minute."

"Good. I suggest you leave your rifle here. It won't do much good down there except for a club."

"I understand. I have my sword I can use if things get real close."

"Jist make sure the damn thing's tied down tight. We don't need you clankin' your way down into the canyon."

"I made sure of that already," Mad Buffalo said. "Now quit your jabberin' and let's git a move on."

Within minutes, Hudson, Mad Buffalo, and Lowell were heading down the treacherous, dizzyingly twisted trail into the canyon. The five other soldiers remained behind on the mesa with Stolen Back Woman, the two Mexican women, and the animals.

Two heart-stopping hours later, the three men stood on the floor of the canyon, breathing heavily.

"Lord Almighty, I ain't ever seen the like," Linus breathed.

"Jist be glad we did it at night, Sergeant," Hudson said with a low chuckle.

"Why?"

"This way you didn't have to see what you was doin', boy. You had to come down there lookin' over the edge of that damn trail, you'd have shit your britches."

Lowell smiled into the darkness. "I think you're probably right, Linus."

"Let's move," Hudson said, mind back on the business at hand.

There was but a small sliver of moon, but the thick blanket of stars provided some light to move by, now that they were out of the shadow of the steep cliff. It helped, too, that the ground was mostly open, except for sage and other brush. Even if they had been unable to see anything at all, the barking of dogs would have guided them. The three men moved with a fair amount of speed until they were nearing the village itself. Then they slowed.

Crouching behind a palo duro tree, Hudson asked in a whisper, "You know what lodge they're in, Mad Buffalo?"

"Two of 'em's in one lodge, but the third's in another."

"You know which lodges?"

"I think so. Might be hard tellin' down here in the dark, though."

"We'll find out. Sergeant, you'll have to talk with your boys in there. Let 'em know who you are. I'll help you. Mad Buffalo'll take care of any troubles the Comanches might think to spring on us. I'll join him in a hurry if it seems necessary. Ready?"

"Yes." Lowell found that his mouth was dry and his hands were wet. "Lead on, my friend," he said to Mad Buffalo.

They moved silently past tipis and fires. Even Lowell managed to make almost no noise. Several dogs came up to sniff and snarl at them, but Mad Buffalo growled back in Comanche, telling them to get away. It worked. The dogs were still rather suspicious since their sense of smell told them that these three men were not of this place, but the insistence in Mad Buffalo's voice and the familiar words sent them slinking off anyway.

They roamed a little as Mad Buffalo tried to get his bearings, but he did after a few minutes. He finally stopped at one large lodge. Hudson eased the flap open a little, and Mad Buffalo slipped inside. Lowell followed, face coated with sweat, heart thumping. Hudson was the last in and he shut the flap. The three paused to let their eyes adjust to the lodge, which had some light from the low fire.

Mad Buffalo tapped Hudson on the shoulder and pointed twice. The white man nodded and pointed them out to Lowell. Then the two whites moved forward, heading toward the farthest away of the soldiers. When Lowell nodded that he was ready, Hudson slapped one hard, strong hand over the sleeping soldier's mouth and the other on his chest.

The soldier jerked awake, eyes wide with terror. Lowell bent right next to his ear. "I'm Sergeant Alfred Lowell, First Dragoons. We come to get you out of here. Understand?"

The soldier nodded, still fearful.

"You got boots?" Lowell whispered. When the soldier nodded, Lowell added, "When Mister Hudson here lets you loose, get up and get your boots on. Then stay here and don't make a goddamn sound."

Once more came the nod and Hudson released him. Still frightened, the soldier sat up and reached for his boots. He was somewhat reassured to actually be able to see Lowell and to see that the powerful man who had held him down also was white, though not an army man.

Lowell and Hudson moved ever so quietly to the other soldier and went through the ritual again. Within minutes, both troopers had their boots on. Then one spotted Mad Buffalo. His eyes grew wide and his mouth opened. Hudson gave him a black look of warning and the man shut his mouth.

Hudson moved out of the lodge, took a look around and then held the flap open. Inside, Lowell jerked his head at the two captive soldiers. They moved swiftly out, making more noise than Lowell felt comfortable with. But the sleeping Comanches seemed oblivious. Then Lowell went out, followed by Mad Buffalo.

"You know where your friend is?" Hudson asked. He was sure Mad Buffalo could find the other lodge, but the soldiers should know where it was and would save them some time. The longer they were in the village, the greater their chances of being discovered.

"Down toward the river," one soldier said. "I can show you."

CHAPTER 23

The soldier led them swiftly to the lodge where their companion was being held. Once again, Mad Buffalo was the first in, to make sure everything was all right. Then Lowell entered, followed by the two soldiers, who knew that it would be folly to stay outside while the others were in the tipi. Hudson was again last in.

Hudson and Lowell moved straight to the sleeping soldier. They woke him the same way and went through the questions. But as he sat up to get his boots on, he suddenly groaned, as if in pain, and then swore fairly loudly.

Across the lodge, one of the Comanches stirred and then woke. Mad Buffalo was on him in a moment, and clamped his hands on the Comanche's throat, but not before the Comanche had gotten out one sharp word of warning.

"Fuck," Hudson spat. He spun and jumped toward an older warrior, who was next to wake. In moments, the inside of the lodge turned into an abattoir, as

Hudson and Mad Buffalo killed all the Comanches in the tipi, including a small child. They could not afford to have any alarm given to the village.

The former captives sat in rapt wonder as they watched the two men, one red, one white, go about their grisly business with speed and incredible effectiveness. The soldiers did not mind the carnage. Indeed, they appreciated it, considering all they had been through in the past several weeks. They were in awe at Hudson's and Mad Buffalo's proficiency, though.

Finally, the killing stopped. It had not really taken all that long. Hudson and Mad Buffalo looked at each other and shrugged. They could have done nothing else, not that they really regretted what they had done. Except maybe for the so small child. That bothered Hudson.

"We best move," Hudson said after a few moments.

"Let's look around some first," Mad Buffalo said. "Maybe we can find a couple guns or somethin' those blue coats can use."

Hudson nodded, and the entire group searched the tipi swiftly, trying to keep silent while haphazardly tossing blankets and food and whatever else they found. They did come up with two trade rifles and a single-shot pistol, plus shooting bags with the supplies to clean and load them.

Hudson handed each of the former captives a firearm and shooting bag. "You use 'em for anything less than a goddamn absolute necessity and I'll shove it up your ass," he warned. "Now let's git the hell out of here."

They left the lodge the same way they had entered it. Then they moved swiftly through the village, at an angle that would have them past the fringes and on the way toward the cliff trail in the shortest time. They stopped at the foot of the trail for a few minutes to rest.

"How're you boys doin'?" Hudson asked, looking from one former captive to another.

"I'm some weak, but not too bad off," one said. "I can make it."

"Your name, boy?"

"Private Doug Gilcrest." He was tall and thin, but not overly so. Hudson could not see much of his face, except for the bushy mustache.

"And you?" Hudson asked, looking at another trooper.

"Private Burr Brownlee," the man answered in a deep voice. "I'll make it, too." He was a man of medium height, but of wide girth. Little of his size was fat. His forearms, where they stuck out of his rolled-up longjohn shirt, were big and muscular. He also had a shaggy mustache.

"And you?" Hudson asked the last one. He was the one who had made the noise in the last lodge that precipitated the slaughter. Hudson didn't much like the soldier because of that and because he seemed somehow furtive. He was taller than Brownlee but not nearly as wide. Nor was he as tall or as thin as Gilcrest.

"Private Seamus McCafferty. I think I've got stove up ribs," he said in a thick Irish brogue. "That's why I made that noise back there in that goddamn tipi." He paused, then added, "I can't say that I'm sorry those Comanches got killed, but I'm not fond of seeing women and children slaughtered because of me, either."

"It's over with now, boy," Hudson said, his dislike of McCafferty not lessening any, but he could not see making an issue of things now. The man's injured ribs did at least partly explain his furtiveness, though. He was just trying to protect his injury. "You think you can make it?" Hudson asked.

"Where're we going?"

"Up there," Hudson said, pointing.

"Then what?"

"Listen to me, boy," Hudson said roughly. "We been on your trail since you was took by them fuckin' Comanches. Because of your goddamn stupidity, I've lost a good friend and we've all been through some starvin' times. I ain't got the time nor inclination to stand here playin' guessin' games with a dickless shit stick like you. If you cain't make it, I'd rather leave you here than endanger everybody else. If you can make it, or even want to try makin' it out of here, shut your fuckin' mouth and let's move."

"I'll make it," McCafferty said nastily. "And I'll tell you now, lad, I don't like bein' spoken to like that."

"Your likes and dislikes don't mean ass sweat to me, shit stick." He walked a few feet away, battling his anger. Then he beckoned to Mad Buffalo. When the Cheyenne stopped, Hudson said, "I'll lead us up there. I want you to bring up the rear to keep an eye out to see if the Comanches come after us. But if any of them blue coats lags behind or gives you a hard time, pitch his ass over the cliff."

"Be my pleasure," Mad Buffalo said, not meaning it too much. He had little liking for any of the blue coats who until a few minutes ago were Comanche captives, but he wouldn't want to toss one of them to his death. At least not yet. He had a feeling that the three men would drive him to that point before too long.

"Let's go," Hudson said, heading up the trail. He wanted to sprint to the top, giving them all more time to get away, but he knew the recent captives would not be able to keep up, so he took his time, moving steadily but not too quickly.

Going up the trail was infinitely harder than it had been going down. The trek was made worse with the three recent captives being as weak as they were. About halfway up, McCafferty was puffing and having trouble keeping up, and Lowell went back to help him. Brownlee and Gilcrest did as well as could be expected but Hudson still worried about the time. It seemed to be taking forever to get anywhere.

The six made it to the top of the mesa just about dawn. They hurried across the flat, with Hudson calling softly every few steps, "Private O'Murray. It's us."

O'Murray, whom Lowell had left in charge, finally heard it. "Come on in, Mister Hudson," he said. "The others with you?"

"Yep."

O'Murray nodded with satisfaction when he spotted six figures instead of three moving toward him in the growing light.

Gilcrest, Brownlee, and McCafferty stopped in their tracks when they spotted the two Mexican women.

"Never thought you'd see them again, did you, boys?" Hudson said harshly. His disgust for the soldiers overrode any sympathy he might've had for them because of their captivity. In the light of the new day, he could see that the three were battered and bruised. All three were sunburned heavily. Their uniform pants and longjohn shirts were threadbare and ripped. Still, Hudson had seen men in far worse shape who had made out all right.

"No," Gilcrest said, voice faint.

"Well, we got 'em back from some other Comanche band, shit stick. Of course, the third one you boys tried to debase was killed back at the beginning."

"We didn't try to ..." Brownlee said angrily, but he stopped at Hudson's harsh voice.

"You're a lyin' sack of shit," Hudson hissed, "and we all know it. Now, I'm gonna tell you what I promised these women. You so much as look at 'em crossways and you'll regret it."

"We will, huh?" Brownlee said a little arrogantly.

"Yep."

"What're you gonna do?" Brownlee sneered. Now that he was free, he figured he was in Lowell's custody and a sergeant in the U.S. Army would not let some rank old mountain man and scout harm a soldier.

"I'll cut your puny little balls off and shove 'em down your throat."

"And I'll help him," Lowell said roughly.

Brownlee's cockiness dropped off him like a

stone when he saw the look of sincerity on Lowell's face. "You really mean that, Sarge?"

"What do you think, asshole?"

"For a couple goddamn Mexicans?" Brownlee asked, incredulous.

"They're women, Private. It don't matter that they're Mexican."

"We're at war with Mexico, Sarge," Gilcrest said quietly.

"And that gives you the right to rape women of that nation? Even ones who're married to men who work for the man who was good enough to open his fort to the Army of the West?"

"Well, we didn't know ..." Gilcrest tried.

"Bullshit. Now, you heed Mister Hudson's words or you'll never get back to Bent's Fort to face your punishment."

Mad Buffalo had wandered off while the white men were arguing. Suddenly, he came trotting back. Hudson spun to face him.

"The village's awake," he said. "And they've found that the prisoners are missin'—and that there's a lodge full of bodies down there."

"I reckon we ought to git our asses out of here, eh," Hudson said with a touch of sarcasm.

"That'd be wise," Lowell said dryly.

Hudson turned to Mad Buffalo again. "Go on back over by the rim and keep an eye out for those shit sticks. They start comin' up the trail in the next few minutes, we're gonna be in some big ass trouble."

Mad Buffalo nodded. Before he could move, though, Stolen Back Woman brought him his pony.

Mad Buffalo nodded thanks and jumped on. Then he galloped over to the rim and kept watch.

As soon as they had heard Mad Buffalo's pronouncement, the other men had leaped into work, saddling horses and hastily gathering and packing supplies. Within minutes, they were about ready.

"Take those ponies," Lowell ordered Gilcrest, Brownlee and McCafferty. He pointed.

The three privates knew better than to argue here and now. Even if they wanted to, the thought of a whole village of Comanches coming after them would be enough to stop any argument before it started.

Mad Buffalo, who had been casting occasional glances at the group while still keeping an eye on the Comanches, noted that the group was about ready to leave. He galloped over there.

"They comin?" Hudson asked.

"Not yet. Looks like a lot of confusion down there. Probably figure their medicine's gone bad."

"That ain't gonna hold 'em long."

"Nope. But it gives us some time."

"We best make the best use of it, too," Hudson said as he helped Stolen Back Woman onto her pony.

Mad Buffalo could not see that such a statement needed a response, so he didn't make one.

O'Murray helped Lourdes Garcia onto a horse, then mounted his own. Hochner did the same for Guadalupe Sanchez.

Hudson took a swift look around. Then he nodded. "Lead us out of here, Mad Buffler," Hudson said. "Pronto."

Hudson and his strange group rode off, pushing

as hard as they could, knowing that the Comanches would not be far behind them. Their mounts were tired, though, and they didn't move nearly as fast as Hudson would have liked.

Mad Buffalo rode out ahead, but it was less than a hundred yards. He led them about due west until they were off the mesa beyond the edge of the canyon. At the first opportunity, he swung northwest.

They stopped for half an hour around noon, bolting down jerky or pemmican and letting the animals breathe and rest. Then they were moving again, though more slowly.

"Can't we pick up the pace any, Linus?" Lowell asked shortly after they left their nooning spot. He had ridden back to where Hudson was in the unaccustomed position of bringing up the rear.

"Sure," Hudson said with a nod. "If you want to run the risk of killin' half the animals and puttin' us all on foot." He glanced at Lowell riding beside him. "Don't worry too much about it, Sergeant," he added. "They'll either catch us or they won't. I've been watching behind us—that's why I'm ridin' back here—and I ain't seen no sign of any pursuit."

"Maybe they think their medicine's gone bad enough that they won't come after us," Lowell said hopefully.

"Ain't likely."

Hudson decided as darkness was falling that they needed to stop. The three soldiers who had been captured were worn down and weak; the two senoras were exhausted and almost completely dispirited. The other soldiers weren't in much better shape. They were sick of the constant riding, the ever-present dangers that lurked all about them, and they were mighty tired.

All of them knew the potential danger of stopping but all were willing to risk it for some rest. Since they were fairly certain the Comanches would be tracking them sooner or later, they wanted at least some food and rest to try to build up their reserves for when the battle came.

Deciding to take another risk, Hudson told Lowell to have a couple of his soldiers dig a hole about two feet in diameter and about the same deep. Lowell looked at him strangely but he could tell by Hudson's face that the former mountain man was not interested in hearing—or answering—questions. He gave the orders.

Soon after, Stolen Back Woman had a buffalo chip fire built in the hole. She had deer meat that Mad Buffalo had brought in cooking and coffee boiling. The men lolled about after their chores were done, waiting with expectation for their meal to be done. The two Mexican women sat off to themselves a little, Lourdes's arm protectively around Guadalupe's shoulders.

Hudson, Mad Buffalo, and Lowell sat near the fire, but, not close enough to get in Stolen Back Woman's way. "Why does Mad Buffalo do all the huntin', Linus?" Lowell asked. "I've seen you shoot and you're damned good."

"Mad Buffalo hunts with a bow."

"So?" A pause, then, "Of course, no sound, unlike a firearm. The noise might give us away."

"Yep."

All the men took turns standing watch for the night. In the morning, just after finishing off the deer meat, the soldiers began preparing to leave. Mad Buffalo and Hudson rode southeast, along their back trail. They still saw no signs of pursuit, but both were uneasy, their instincts telling them the Comanches were coming and knowing they could not outrun them.

They pushed as hard as they dared, but by late morning Hudson knew the Comanches were coming. He had seen the cloud of dust behind them and followed its progress for a while, hoping they could find some kind of haven or defensible place to make a stand.

An hour later, when they had reached the Canadian River, Hudson called a halt. "Them shit sticks're on their way, and there ain't no better place we can make a stand," he announced. "At least not anywhere we can git to. And this'll give us some time to prepare for them boys."

There was little vegetation left in the area, obviously having been destroyed recently by fire. Still, the group threw up fortifications using what brush, small shrunken logs, dirt, and rocks they could find. It wasn't much, and they were still rather exposed but it was the best they could do. They did have the river at their backs, giving them protection from that side, which helped.

So, having done what they could, they settled in to await the arrival of the Comanches. They did not have long to wait.

CHAPTER 24

The Comanches came hard across the rolling flats, not knowing that Hudson's group had decided to make a stand at the Canadian River. The enemy warriors appeared and disappeared as they rode the lightly undulating land. When the Comanches were within a quarter of a mile of Hudson and his group, Hudson said loudly, "Don't nobody fire till I say so."

When the Comanches were only about a hundred yards off, Hudson roared, "Now!" He fired his old Hawken and noted that a warrior went down, and then lay unmoving after he stopped bouncing.

The soldiers fired with good effect, knocking down three more Comanches. One of those got up and a fellow warrior whisked the wounded man onto the back of his own pony.

The Comanches reacted quickly and before the sound of the soldiers' gunfire had drifted across the plains, the Indians were racing back the way they had just come. They paused only long enough to scoop up their fallen comrades.

Hudson got off three shots with his Hawken and dropped another Comanche, plus a pony. Then the Comanches were pretty much out of range, several hundred yards away, sitting on top of a low ridge.

"Troops, report!" Lowell barked.

Each soldier answered with a "fine" or an "all right, Sergeant."

Then O'Murray crowed, "That's showin' them sons of bitches!"

"Sure was," Hudson agreed. "But they ain't gonna be unsuspectin' the next time."

"You think there'll be a next time?" Lowell called out. "Maybe we've broken their medicine good and proper this time."

"Might be," Hudson allowed. "But it ain't likely. Not yet anyway." He looked back toward the river. Everything seemed fine back there. Private Butterworth was watching the horses, being helped by Stolen Back Woman. Lourdes and Guadalupe were back there, too, sitting along the riverbank. Hudson had figured it was as safe a place as they were going to find here. He had to admit, though, that he was just a bit annoyed with them for not having volunteered to do something to help out here. He pushed that thought from his mind as he turned his head again to watch the Comanches. The two women had been through some horrible times and were still too scared and dispirited to do much but sit and stare, wondering what would happen to them next.

"Hey, Linus," Lowell called after a few minutes.

"Does it seem to you that there ain't as many of those Comanches out there now?"

Hudson stared for a while, then said, "Yep."

"Where'd they go?"

"Down behind the ridge, I reckon."

"What for?"

"I reckon some of them shit sticks're plannin' to move upriver and downriver a little to come at us from the flanks. The rest'll come at us head on, figurin' we'll be concentrating on them. Then those others'll surprise us. Or so I figure they're thinkin'."

"If that's true, it leaves us is a bad position, don't it?" Lowell asked.

"Shit," Hudson snorted. "We been in a piss poor position since we left Bent's place. One thing that's in our favor, though, is that we know what those shit sticks're gonna do—if I've figured it right."

"We gonna do anything about it?"

"Set a little reception for 'em," Hudson said grimly. He rose and walked to Lowell's position and crouched. "You wait here and keep watch on those Comanches out there, Sergeant," he said. "If they charge, we'll know the others'll be comin' at us right off. I want you to place half your men on each flank—not far, though; maybe five or six yards is all. You, me, and Mad Buffalo'll hold the front."

"There's an uneven number of men available, what with Private Butterworth watchin' the horses."

"I'll take care of that." He moved through the haven toward the horses. "Go report to Sergeant Lowell," he commanded the soldier, who nodded and hurried off. Hudson knelt in front of the two Mexican women. "You senoras want any chance of gittin' out of this mess alive, you're gonna have to help out."

Eyes wide with fright, Lourdes asked, "What can we do?"

"Help Stolen Back Woman tend to the horses."

"No!" Lourdes gasped. She was reluctant to say she wanted nothing to do with the Cheyenne woman or any other Indian.

"Listen to me, senora," Hudson said harshly. "There's only eleven of us to fight, against maybe thirty Comanches. The numbers ain't good. Now you ain't some fancy wives of the ricos down in Taos. You're common folk jist like the rest of us. You can watch over horses."

"But..."

"No buts, senora. I know you don't want to be with Stolen Back Woman because she's an Injin, but your wants don't matter much right now. You don't help us out now, I'll cast you out to those goddamn demons out there again. You want that?"

"You wouldn't!" Lourdes exploded, terror clutching at her heart. But she could see in his face and eyes that he would do just what he said.

"Now, you don't have to hold Stolen Back Woman's hand, though God knows, she's done far more'n she should've to try to git in your good graces. Jist keep the horses from bein' took or run off."

Lourdes nodded. She was still frightened to death but the alternative was even worse to contemplate. She spoke to Guadalupe in Spanish and then the two women rose and walked tentatively toward the horses.

Hudson went back to Lowell. "Everything set, Sergeant?" he asked.

"Yes. Private O'Murray's in charge on the right flank, with Privates McCafferty, Hogg, and McKagan. Private Hochner's on the left, in charge of Privates Butterworth, Brownlee, and Gilcrest."

Hudson nodded and headed back to his position, wondering where Mad Buffalo was. He knew the Cheyenne was around somewhere but he could never keep track of the warrior at times like this. Mad Buffalo had the ability to melt into the background wherever he was.

It was more than an hour before the Comanches came at the small group again. They came silently, crouched over their ponies, firing arrows when they got close enough. They made small, hard to hit targets and Hudson had warned the men not to waste precious powder and ball by shooting too many horses. They dropped a few ponies, hoping that would kill the Comanche riders but it was difficult to tell if they had any success.

Then came O'Murray's shout from the right flank of, "Here they come," followed moments later by the same from Hochner on the left. Those Comanches who were attacking on the ends got a rude surprise when they found the soldiers waiting for them. While there were only four troopers on each side, the Comanches had lost the element of surprise and that helped even the odds some, even if only a little.

Then Comanches were flooding into the small haven from three sides. Most of them were on foot, though a few were still mounted. Hudson jumped up from behind his small breastworks, fully loaded Colts in his hand. He let out a whoop and fired both revolvers until they were empty before casting them aside.

A mounted Comanche charged at him and he ducked as the warrior swung a war club at him. He managed to grab the Indian's arm and jerk the Comanche down from the pony. With a swift tug and spin, he snapped the warrior's arm. He kicked the Indian in the face, then yanked out his tomahawk and split open his chest with it.

Hudson whirled just in time to have another warrior swing a knife at him. The blade ripped through Hudson's cloth shirt and opened a long, ragged cut across his chest and the top of his abdomen. As the Comanche reached back to stab him, Hudson kicked the Indian in the groin and then chopped him across the neck with his tomahawk.

He looked around, breathing heavily. He saw the soldiers on each flank fighting almost desperately. Then he spotted Mad Buffalo flitting through the camp like a bloodthirsty wraith. The Cheyenne was fighting with all the abandon of the animal for which he was named.

Hudson waded back into the battle, slashing and hacking at any Comanche he came across, fighting with an almost maniacal fury as thoughts of Whirling Storm's death at the hands of the Comanches swept over him. Now was the time for revenge. The captive women had been rescued, as had the captive soldiers. The Mexican soldados had been punished and now it was time for the Comanches to pay for all the evil they had done of late.

The soldiers, seeing the fury of the Cheyenne and

the former mountain man, were impressed, and they increased their efforts even more.

In a stolen moment of rest, Hudson saw Stolen Back Woman taking part in the fray. She had evidently just shot one of the Comanches down with her own small Colt Paterson and she was moving toward Butterworth, who was struggling with a pudgy, strong Comanche. Another Comanche was creeping toward Butterworth from his blind side. Just as that warrior raised his war club to brain Butterworth, Stolen Back Woman skidded to a stop and fired twice.

Butterworth flung his opponent to the ground and spun, worried. He saw the dead Comanche and Stolen Back Woman with the smoking pistol in her hand. He grinned. "Much obliged, ma'am," he said. Then he turned and ran for O'Murray, who was fending off two warriors.

Stolen Back Woman glanced at Hudson, who smiled and nodded. Then he turned to help Lowell, who had an arrow sticking out of his side and was trying to battle a short, broad warrior. Within seconds, Hudson had slain the Comanche and helped Lowell to sit. "How bad is it, Sergeant?" he asked urgently.

"Not too bad," Lowell answered with a grimace. "I don't think it went in too deep."

"Stay here and out of the way, if you can," Hudson ordered as he rose and dashed off into the confusion of the battle.

He was no longer needed, though. The Comanches had broken off the engagement. The ones who could were mounted on their ponies and racing across the plains. Some carried dead or wounded companions with them but they did leave a few bodies scattered about the white men's camp.

Mad Buffalo suddenly materialized next to Hudson. "Chickenshits," the Cheyenne muttered.

Hudson looked at him and saw the blood. "You're hurt?" he asked, worried. That's all he needed now was to have Mad Buffalo go under on him.

"Couple small stab wounds. They don't mean shit."

"You sure?"

"Yep."

Hudson nodded. Then he headed for the left flank to check on the soldiers there. Hogg was dead, and the three others had been wounded, none seriously. Then Hudson checked the other flank. Everyone there had sustained a wound of some sort, but only one of the men—McCafferty— looked to be in bad shape.

Hudson finally headed back to the women and horses. The animals were all there and there were two Comanche ponies added to the herd.

All three women were unharmed, though Stolen Back Woman laughingly showed Hudson where a Comanche arrow had cut across the seat of her dress. "Didn't even break the skin," she said, still laughing.

Hudson grabbed her, pulled her close and then cupped her soft buttocks in his hands and squeezed them. "Good goddamn thing, too," he said. "This ol' boy likes your ass jist the way it is."

Hudson broke away from Stolen Back Woman, winked at her, and then headed back to where Lowell and Mad Buffalo were waiting. The sergeant was still sitting, contemplating the arrow in his side with mystified wonder. "That's got to come out sooner or later, Sergeant," Hudson said with a grin.

"I was afraid you were gonna say that, Linus," Lowell said with a grimace of irritation. "But I figure it can wait till this ruckus is finally over." He paused. "It ain't over, is it?" he asked, a little disheartened.

"It seem to be over, Mad Buffalo?" Hudson asked his friend.

"Don't think so. Those chickenshits're sitting on a ridge a far piece out there. Looks like they're tryin' to decide if their medicine still eats shit."

Hudson looked out across the prairie.

"You see that one son of a bitch seems to be shoutin' at the others?" Mad Buffalo asked. When Hudson nodded, he continued. "He seems to be the war chief for this fractious group. Looks to me like the old fart's trying to fire 'em up to make another run at us."

"Maybe it's time to put an end to this shit," Hudson said quietly.

"What're you gonna do, Linus?" Lowell asked as Hudson began walking off.

"You'll see," Hudson said over his shoulder. He picked up his rifle and cleaned it carefully, wanting to make sure the barrel was not fouled at all. Then he took extreme care in loading it, using an extra-heavy dose of powder. Then he walked out onto the prairie a little way. Mad Buffalo and Lowell followed him, the Cheyenne helping the soldier.

"Come here, my friend," Hudson said in Cheyenne.

Mad Buffalo slipped out from under Lowell's arm, leaving him standing alone, wondering. "What do you need, my friend?" the Cheyenne asked in his own language. He knew this was serious by the way Hudson had spoken.

"I aim to use you as a gun rest," Hudson said in English since Cheyenne was inadequate for such words. Mad Buffalo nodded. "You want to face me or them shit sticks out there?" His lips twitched a little. "I know you'd ruther look at my handsome face, but with this ol' Hawken goin' off in your face, you might want to be lookin' away."

"Away'll shine. I look at your ugly face and I jist might flinch when you shoot."

"You best not flinch one way or the other," Hudson said in mock harshness.

Mad Buffalo nodded solemnly and turned. Hudson rested the barrel of the Hawken on Mad Buffalo's right shoulder.

"What the hell're you gonna do?" Lowell asked, mystified and more than a little worried.

"Shoot that shitstick war chief out there," Hudson said flatly.

"Goddamn, Linus, he's got to be five hundred yards away," Lowell said with wide eyes.

"I figure more like six hundred."

"You can't hit a target at that range."

"The hell I cain't.

"Even if you do, you ain't gonna kill him."

"Might. Might not. But it don't matter none. I hit him from this range and those Comanches'll be gone. That'd show my medicine's far too strong for them wretches."

"But..."

"Jist shut up and watch, boy," Hudson growled. He bent and aimed taking plenty of time. He adjusted his sights several times and wiped his hands off twice. Then he said softly. "Git ready."

Mad Buffalo stiffened and stood as if made of stone.

Hudson fired and then slowly straightened. It was a heart-stopping few seconds, but then the Comanche war chief fell off his horse.

"Jesus goddamn Christ," O'Murray breathed. He and all the rest of the soldiers had noticed something was going on and moved up to watch. "What a goddamn shot."

The Comanches on the ridge dismounted and huddled around the fallen figure. Stolen Back Woman moved up alongside Hudson and handed him his telescope. The former mountain man looked first and then let the rest of the men peer through it.

After a few minutes, the Comanches lifted the war chiefs body into the arms of a mounted warrior. Then the rest jumped on their ponies. Each seemed to look toward the white men but they made no taunts. They turned and galloped off the far side of the ridge.

"They gone for good?" Gilcrest asked.

"I reckon so," Hudson said.

Mad Buffalo finally turned. He was grinning. "You ain't so bad with that goddamn smoke pole, my friend," he said.

"I keep tellin' you that."

"I'll go see if they're really gone," Mad Buffalo said, heading for the herd. He returned in just over a half an hour. "They're movin' so fast I couldn't keep up with 'em," Mad Buffalo said as he dismounted. "I don't figure they'll be back."

While Mad Buffalo had been gone, Stolen Back Woman, Lourdes, and Guadalupe had patched up the men as best they could and then made food and coffee. Since the possibility of the Comanches returning any time soon was so remote, Hudson decided they would stay there for the night.

In the morning, weary and wounded, but full of spirit, Hudson and his small group began their trek back to Bent's Fort.

A LOOK AT:
SHERIFF'S BLOOD ROCKY MOUNTAIN LAWMEN BOOK 1

Jonas Culpepper is the no-nonsense sheriff of San Juan County in Colorado, patrolling the vast empty lands with his 200-pound mastiff, Bear. His dedication has won him the respect of everyone on the right side of the law. But he is a fierce and relentless foe of those who cross him or those he has sworn to protect. So when the Durango-Silverton train is robbed by Mack Ellsworth and his gang of villains, it is Culpepper's duty to run them down and bring them to justice. But his job is made all the more dangerous when his enemies include men on both sides of the law. And when Culpepper's wife is kidnapped, hell comes to San Juan County in the form of one enraged lawman.

AVAILABLE NOW

ABOUT THE AUTHOR

John Legg has published more than 55 novels, all on Old West themes. Blood of the Scalphunter is his latest novel in the field of his main interest — the Rocky Mountain Fur Trade. He first wrote of the fur trade in Cheyenne Lance, his initial work.

Cheyenne Lance and Medicine Wagon were published while Legg was acquiring a B.A. in Communications and an M.S. in Journalism. Legg has continued his journalism career, and is a copy editor with The New York Times News Service.

Since his first two books, Legg has, under his own name, entertained the Western audience with many more tales of man's fight for independence on the Western frontier. In addition, he has had published several historical novels set in the Old West. Among those are War at Bent's Fort and Blood at Fort Bridger.

In addition, Legg has, under pseudonyms, contributed to the Ramseys, a series that was published by Berkley, and was the sole author of the eight books in the Saddle Tramp series for HarperPaperbacks. He also was the sole author of Wildgun, an eight-book adult Western series from Berkley/Jove. He also has published numerous articles and a nonfiction book — Shinin' Trails: A Possibles Bag of Fur Trade History — on the subject,

He is member of Western Fictioneers.

In addition, he operates JL TextWorks, an editing/critiquing service.